SILK AND SHADOWS

THE VIRGIN DIARIES

LAUREN LANDISH

Edited by
VALORIE CLIFTON
Edited by
STACI ETHERIDGE

PROLOGUE

NORMA

*D*ear Diary,

I'm doing it. I'm on my way to the top, just like I planned. Now, the university newspaper, and later, some serious investigative journalism. Business . . . or maybe politics? I'm not sure just yet, but I know I'm going to get there.

My focus is sharp, honed through an obsession with hard work and an unwillingness to fail that I learned at the elbows of two of the greatest men I know, my father and my brother.

Unfortunately, they're the only men in my life. My sharp tongue and quick wit are usually a turnoff for most guys, their inability to handle a mouthy woman usually apparent before we even get to a first date. But I'm not going to change for anyone. The right man for me will match me word for word, biting retort for biting retort, and together, we'll challenge each other to be better.

At least that's the plan. But honestly, I'm not sure he even exists. If not, I'll probably stay a single virgin forever, no compromise, no wavering. I'll be true to who I am . . . even if that means I'm alone with only my work to fulfill me.

CHAPTER 1

NORMA

*T*o say I slept like hell last night would be an understatement. I love my barely off-campus apartment and the fact that I can live alone, unlike most sophomores on campus, but the building's cheap walls are paper-thin. So thin that I might as well have a roommate, a freakishly loud one in the apartment next door who was moaning and groaning for hours last night. I mean, seriously, who lets their headboard thump against the wall while screaming 'yes' over and over . . . for *hours*? After that long, I'm thinking it's not really gonna happen for you and you should give up so the rest of the world can get some sleep before morning classes. Inconsiderate skank. Yes, skank because the girl in question once shared, unprompted, mind you, that she learned to never yell the guys' names because she got it wrong one time. Shudder. I can't imagine not knowing the name of the person literally inside you. So yeah, inconsiderate skank.

But maybe I just wouldn't get it? I've rarely dated and

have only been to second base a time or two, but I most definitely know the names of those guys. When my neighbor had first moved in, it'd been a naughty tease to listen to her nightly play by play, and in the privacy of my own place, I'd quietly gone along with it, using my fingers or the occasional toy.

But now, I usually end up sleeping on my couch in an attempt to put more walls and more space between her auditory assault and me.

Hence, the reason I slept like hell. My couch isn't that comfy, making me doubly grumpy from lack of sleep and an abysmally poor quality of sleep. My dad or my brother would willingly pay for me to stay at a nicer place where I wouldn't have to deal with this, but I'm a stubborn girl.

So off to the school paper I go, the only possible bright spot that could shove me out of this funk. Or so I hope.

Those hopes are quickly dashed at Erica's words.

"You want me to *what*?" I screech, though I'm trying to keep my voice down a bit so that the other employees don't prairie-dog out of their cubbies to see what's going on. They'd probably volunteer for any assignment Erica would throw their way. But not this. For the love of God, not this.

Erica, the editor at *The Chronicle* and better known as my boss, stares at me like I asked why I need to be the one to cure cancer. Honestly, I think curing cancer might be easier. "Look, Norma, I know it's a big request, but you're the best person for this assignment."

This 'assignment' is tutoring the star quarterback of our football team, something completely out of my wheelhouse. Also, it's something I don't have time for with my own studies and constantly working to find stories that will get me bylines in the paper. I give her a bit of a glare, tempering it only because she's the senior in charge and I'm a newly-hired and lowly sophomore.

"Seriously, the school got a major black eye last year when the star of the basketball team lost his eligibility right at the end of the season. That cost us big time. And Coach Jefferson isn't willing to gamble like that. If the football team is going anywhere near a bowl game this season, he needs Zach Knight holding the ball. And for that to happen, he has to pass English." She's whispering, like the idea that a football jock might not be good in the classroom is some big newsflash.

"Okay, I get that, but English?" I reply. "Why not get an English major to tutor him?"

Erica's eyes drop, instantly letting me know that there's more to the story coming. I brace myself because judging by the way she's hemming and hawing, this is bad. "Well, Coach asked for a favor." That doesn't surprise me. Erica does a great job highlighting our football team and has been rewarded with some private interviews in return, so she's got a 'scratch my back and I'll scratch yours' deal with Coach Jefferson. "It's not just that Zach needs a tutor. He needs a tutor on the down low. No one can know about this. No. One. And while you're new here, I've been impressed with your ability to protect your sources. So, I'm trusting that you'll keep your mouth shut about this."

There's no threat hanging in the air, just like there's no promise of me getting a leg up at *The Chronicle* if I do this and succeed. But still, the implications are clear. If I help Zach, I'm making a back-scratch agreement with Erica too, and she upholds those under-the-table deals as much as she can. If I don't do this . . . well, I can't imagine that'd work in my favor.

I sigh, arching an eyebrow. "Fine, you know I'm going to do this. But I need to know . . . why the secrecy? Most of the players have tutors. Hell, it's common knowledge that a few of them basically pay people to take their classes for them. Why's this one such a big deal?"

Erica looks around like she's afraid someone is listening in on our conversation, and I wonder why this is what's setting her off, considering everything else she just said. "Do you follow our football team at all?" I shake my head. Past the fact that I could recognize a football, I'm pretty clueless. She sighs, gathering her thoughts. "Okay, so our team is at a crossroads. Zach is a top-notch player, likely pro-quality. So with him on the field, we're a shoe-in for a bowl game. That translates to money, something I *know* you understand."

I nod, though I try to keep my family's wealth out of the picture at school, not needing any attention for something that has nothing to do with me. But Erica knows because of the article I wrote about my bigshot CEO brother, Liam.

But I know that football and colleges go together like money and . . . money. Few of the players, in any of the top sports, are here because they're academically gifted, but because they make money for the school. I'm not bitter about that, though. It takes all kinds to make the world go 'round, and I've gotta give it to the guys who work their asses off to use their talent on the field to get a piece of paper most folks would kill for.

"So, if there's a question as to his eligibility, the money machine that is 'football' around here could grind to a halt. No one wants to watch second-string guys play. They want to watch greatness on the cusp of something even greater . . . and that's Zach. The athletic director already had to pull some strings with the dean so that Zach can maintain eligibility for now, but that's a temporary solution until you help him." Her eyes plead with me to understand what she's saying. "Coach said that there's a lot of pressure for quarterbacks with pro scouts too. The scouts want guys who are good on the field, but these days, QBs are team reps, so they need to be good-looking, well-spoken, and relatively intelligent. So if word gets out that Zach, while he's definitely good on the field and gorgeous, is as dumb as a rock and might be putting the entire season for the team in jeopardy, it'll start a chain reaction of bad news for the school, Coach, and even Zach. Do you get what I'm saying?"

I let her words mull over in my mind. "Just to be clear, though, I'm not doing his work *for* him. I'll tutor him, but he's going to have to study *himself*, do the papers *himself*, and take the tests *himself*. I will tutor him. I'm not taking his English class for him."

Erica sighs in relief. "Of course. That's all I'm asking, Norma. But there is one more teeny-tiny piece to the puzzle." She holds up her finger and thumb an inch apart.

I look at her expectantly, decidedly not liking the look of horror on her face and the way she's not looking me in the eye now. "What, Erica? How bad is it?"

She takes a breath, fortifying herself, and then whispers, "Coach is concerned that even if you keep your mouth shut, there's a risk that this could all be found out. Zach's the star so people pay attention to who he's seen with. So he wants a . . . cover story, if you will. I need you to basically be undercover as his tutor. It'll be good practice for when you actually are an investigative journalist."

She's rambling a bit and I'm not quite following her train of thought. "And my cover would be . . .?" I prompt.

Her eyes meet mine. "Zach Knight's girlfriend."

My mouth drops in shock. "What the hell, Erica? Absolutely not! That's ridiculous. I'll just tutor him discreetly and it won't even be a big deal. Happens all the time."

But even as I protest, Erica is shaking her head. "No, Norma. You have to. Please. It's just so no one will question you two hanging out together. Nothing more. People who date hang out together at the library for study dates. And just for a little while, until his grades are up. The faster you get his GPA in check, the sooner you can be done with the whole scam. But this is make-or-break for Zach, and probably for the school. And us too, if we can pull this off for Coach."

She's laying it on thick, guilt-tripping me while simultaneously digging at my school spirit. But my parents made sure that I was made of sturdier stuff than that and I won't be forced into something this crazy. However, one thing I also know is that sometimes, the best opportunities come in really shitty plain-brown packages. And I think this might be one of those times. I'm willing to tutor Zach—that's not an issue—and if I have to go to a few games and wear his jersey to sell the lie, what's the harm? It's not like I'm busy with a real boyfriend anyway.

And the potential rewards could be great. I'll have an in with Erica and Coach Jefferson, and the undercover practice might help down the road.

I narrow my eyes. "Okay. I'll do it. But this is a big favor and I want you to know that I recognize that."

Erica looks relieved. "Thank you. I won't forget this."

I look her square in the eye, a lesson I learned long ago from my dad. "I won't either, Erica." I let a pause lengthen to add impact to my words before continuing, "So, when does covert operation 'Save the Jock' begin?"

"Today. Luckily, the team had today off from field practice so you're meeting with Zach at five at the library. Be there and be square. Good luck. We're counting on you." Erica breaks out into a huge grin and I can't help but feel I just got played a bit.

But I know that I'm new, and being agreeable, even when it's something as crazy as being a fake girlfriend to hide the fact that I'm tutoring a football player, can only help me on my path. Helping Zach helps me.

I try to remember that as I search my brain for what I know about our football team and Zach Knight. Admittedly, it's not much, but even someone as unaware of sports as I am knows of Zach. Erica called him gorgeous and she's not wrong. Zach is nice eye candy, tall and broad-shouldered, with thick muscles that somehow don't look bulky but are lean, and a face that has lit up our Jumbo Tron more than a few times. Blond hair that he's usually running his fingers through from just taking his helmet off, blue eyes, and a square jaw. He's the quintessential All-American guy, football god and all. And apparently, as of five o'clock, my new fake boyfriend.

FIVE O'CLOCK COMES AND GOES, AND I FEEL LIKE AN idiot standing in the middle of the library foyer, looking for all the world like a girl who just got stood up on a study date. There's no sign of Zach, and I decide not to waste time and to get some of my own studying done while I wait.

There's a piece of me that wants to just leave, mentally telling myself that if he can't even deign to show up on time for me to help him, then he doesn't deserve the help. But this is helping me get ahead too, I remind my inner bitch, so I give in and wait. Looking around, I pick a quiet corner on the first floor where no one will see us carry out his first lesson. If he shows.

I head over to the table, keeping an eye on the main entrance as I pull out my own work, setting up my laptop and opening the textbook I'm reading from. But though my eyes scan, I'm not really seeing the words on the pages. Instead, I'm fuming.

I'm not too surprised that he's late. I figure the entitled ass probably lives by his own clock, not even bothering to give lame excuses but rather assuming everyone will wait on him. Ironically, considering where I'm currently sitting, he wouldn't be wrong in that assumption.

With a sigh, I force my eyes to focus on my own studies and make some good headway, making notes on the entire third chapter of my World History textbook. I do a bit of color coding and formatting so that it's an easier study later and save my progress.

Time seems to have flown by because when I look at the clock, I realize it's well after six. I've seriously waited for this ass for over an hour and he's still a no-show?

This is bullshit, I fume to myself, wondering how I let Erica talk me into this. I shut down my computer and shove it and my book back into my bag. "I should've known," I mutter quietly. Though whispered, my voice takes on a sarcastic edge, the one Liam says can slice and dice an ego at one hundred paces. "Asshole desperately needs help but can't be bothered to actually show up to get it. Fuck that self-entitled prick. He can fail for all I care."

Suddenly, a deep chuckle right behind me interrupts my rant. It's a guy's voice, his faux-supportive anger mimicking me. "Yeah, fuck that self-entitled prick!"

I was told I was meeting a redhead, and when I heard her grumbling about a self-entitled prick, I knew I'd found her. At my statement, she turns around, fire flashing in her eyes. When I said it, I was just seeing if I could get under the skin of the sexy little wood sprite I'd been checking out as I walked across the library, only to discover her griping about me. I was curious to hear her response.

Well, that and I fully expect her to pull a 180 and grovel at my feet like most girls do. Hell, like *everyone* does. I don't ask for it. It's just what happens.

But I'm surprised she's not relenting. She's glaring daggers, even more so now that she recognizes me. Oh, yeah, I can tell she does. Usually, that makes girls go stupid and soft, simpering into puddles at my feet. But not this one. I offer one of my panty-melting smiles, but she scowls fiercely, her baby blues filled to the brim with attitude.

She looks cute as fuck when she's mad. All fiery hair and fair skin, with a few freckles sprinkled across her cheekbones. She's small enough that I could easily pick her up, but she puts off an aura of anger I haven't seen in some of my defensive linemen. She's frighteningly intimidating for such a pretty little thing. The contrast is interesting.

I offer her a hand. "I'm Zach Knight. But I guess you can call me self-entitled prick, if you prefer." I'm joking, not really apologizing but acknowledging in a slightly self-deprecating way that I'm late. It should be enough to soothe her ruffled feathers.

But no. She doesn't flinch under my gaze, the steel in her spine obvious as she takes my hand for a quick shake. "Norma Jean Blackstone. I'm afraid our session was scheduled for five to six, though, so you've missed your opportunity today. Perhaps we can schedule for tomorrow and you can be on time?" Her voice is saccharin sweet, but the barbs are clear as she tilts her head, looking at me expectantly.

A grin forms on the corners of my lips at her refusal to back down and I cross my arms over my chest to resist grabbing a lock of her red hair. My wide stance blocks her from moving around the table to leave. I think the challenge in my stare has something to do with her staying too. *Goddamn. She has bigger balls than some of the guys on the team. I'm either going to kill her or fuck her . . . and I know which I'd prefer.*

At my lack of response, she puts her hands on her hips. I'm sure she thinks she looks menacing, but she looks sexy to me. Like a nerdy nymph. She's waiting for my reaction, certain she's won this round, but I'm just getting started. I get the feeling she is too.

But I let her have this one. I was late, after all, and I get that she's doing me a solid by even being here. Hell, if she'd been over an hour late to meet me, I'd have been long gone. I offer an explanation. "No need to be bratty. The team had the day off, but we still had to lift. I needed to grab a quick shower after. I wanted to do you the favor of not showing up sweaty and stinky." I intentionally poke at her by acting like I was doing *her* the favor. "Sorry, gotta keep the hardware nice and clean."

I glance down pointedly, knowing her eyes will unconsciously follow where mine go. Her blue gaze flicks down to my cock, soft but filling up my jeans with her attention. She tears her eyes away, and I add a tally mark to my column for rattling her. It's a lazy flirtation, but less has resulted in a girl attempting to throw herself at me. But not Norma.

Her face scrunches into a venomous scowl, her annoyance at taking the bait in her eyes. "Please," she fumes, "spare me the details of your dick. I'm sure it's 'sooo big' and you're 'sooo amazing' but I really don't give a shit." She lets her voice pitch high, affecting a vapid Valley Girl cheerleader vibe. I don't interrupt her to tell her that I've heard that exact phrasing before because she obviously means it to be an insult.

I eye her, letting her think I'm considering her attack, but I reply, "You sound like a porn star when you say it like that." I lean in close, whispering, "Can you do it like that later too?"

She growls, like the cutest tiger ever, and her pouty lips twist. "Maybe I will . . . for the guy who shows up on time for our date." Something about the way she says it lets me know that there's no guy, no date. And Coach said he'd made *arrangements* to cover for our study sessions, so surely, she's not really going out with someone. *Liar, liar, take those fiery pants off and let me see if the carpets match the drapes.* My dirty thoughts are disrupted as she continues, "But you're wasting your time, buddy. I'm here to help you with your English class. Take it or leave it. I have exactly thirty minutes until my plans for the night. What will it be?"

I consider whether maybe I'm wrong and she does actually have a date with some fucker after our tutoring session. Oddly, the thought pisses me off, even if this is supposed to be some fake cover story to save my ass. I like this banter, the back and forth of challenging each other. It's new, different, exciting.

"Do you really have a date?" The words pop out before I can stop them and her eyes narrow.

"Why do you care?" she asks, seemingly legitimately bewildered.

I smirk, sensing the upper hand is mine again with that opening. "I'm just trying to picture the guy who gets all this fire to melt underneath him. He must be fucking Teflon with the knives you throw. But I bet a soft Norma is a sight to behold, a rare gift." I look her up and down, trying to imagine her writhing and begging, submissive and sweet. My breath hitches a bit as my heart rate speeds up. Fuck, this girl could count as my cardio for the day and I'm not even fucking her. Yet.

She shuffles on her feet, more affected by my appraisal than I would've expected. She's not scathing me with a flaming retort. No, she seems almost . . . shocked, judging by the way her mouth rounds, her jaw dropping. "Oh." It's more a sound than a word, and I like that I've managed to make her speechless.

I reach up to run my thumb along her full bottom lip, curious whether the red tinge there is lipstick, for some reason hoping it's her natural lip color but knowing it'd look hot wrapped around my cock either way. Her whole countenance is soft for a second, suspended in time and full of sexual tension as I crowd closely enough to feel the heat from her body against mine. Time slows as I see her desire to yield to me, and I know she's not nearly as unaffected by me as she'd lead me to believe.

And the moment snaps.

She comes back to herself and I see the instant switch in her eyes. She steps back, swallowing hard, but the sassiness is back. "That is none of your damn business. This whole ridiculous fake girlfriend thing is just that—*fake*. I'm not some football groupie who's going to fuck you just because you give a nod. I'm better than that. Hell, those girls are better than that too. So keep it in your pants, don't try to get in mine, and we'll be fine. Capiche?"

I grin, the cold dismissal just as hot as the fire. "Brat, don't talk about things you don't know. You have no idea who I'm fucking or how I get them in bed with me. Unless you want me to show you?"

She flinches, but I'm not sure what I said that zinged so

close to home. I replay the words over in my head. Maybe she does want me to show her? That can be arranged, for fucking sure.

Whatever it was, it set her off in a way our previous verbal blows didn't. She's gone all-business on me. "Word is, you need my help so you don't fail and get kicked off the team right when they need you most. The world is bigger than Xs and Os, so stop with the bullshit and let's get started. Twenty-seven minutes now. You in or out?"

The words are on my lips to tell her to take her orders and shove them up her gorgeous little ass. I'm behind on my GPA, but I'm not stupid. English is just mind-numbingly boring for me, always has been. Some people write epics on paper. I write mine in a different way. Doesn't help that my teacher has a hard-on for *Paradise Lost*, which is the most long-winded pain in the ass of all time. I'm not knocking school, but I didn't come to college to wax poetic. I came because I know my life's path. I'm going to make my mark on the field. Football doesn't last forever, and I'll have my degree for when that time comes, but my legacy with the pigskin will always be my greatest joy. I just need a little help to get through this rough patch, which is why I finally came to terms with Coach's orders to get a tutor.

The staring contest is fierce, but she wins easily. Fuck, this minx is killing me, verbally castrating me and challenging me at every turn. Who'd have thought that would be so damn sexy? "In."

She tries to hide her smile, but I can see it tickling her full lips. "Good. Now that I have your attention, let's get a few things clear." She holds up a finger, demonstrating 'one', but all I see is the blush pink covering her short nails, feminine but functional. "You're going to show me some respect. Out there on the field, you might be the king. But that doesn't mean a damn thing to me here. You obviously need help, and I'm going to help you, but only if you're here on time and don't waste mine." She points to the floor, making sure I get the point that I should be at the library at the arranged time. She sounds uppity, like someone's said that to her before.

"Two." She holds up a second finger. "The cover story Erica and Coach Jefferson came up with is ridiculous, but I guess it'll work if there are any questions or suspicions. But it is fake. I'm not fucking you and we're not dating. But I won't be made a fool of either, so don't go flaunting your groupies around while telling folks we're together. Be discreet and I'll do the same."

"Three." A third finger pops up. "Uhm . . . never mind. I think that was all I have. Questions?"

Her words cut, irritatingly bossy, so I revert to what I know. I grab her hand, bringing her still upheld fingers higher in the air and laying a soft kiss to each fingertip before giving her a hard look. "I think you're confused about the situation, but I agree we should be clear. I know this is stupid, and I hate that it's come to this, but I'll do any-fucking-thing for football, even pretend to date some girl I don't know, who's already busting my balls, just so I can stay on the field. I do need help, but I don't need to hear shit from you about what a dumbass I am. Trust me, I already know, and your talking down to me ain't gonna help a damn thing."

She yanks her hand back, holding it to her chest like my kiss hurt her. Her eyes search mine, and I don't look away, forcing myself to stand up to this little spitfire brat.

She looks down first. "You're right. I'm sorry. I didn't mean to be insulting . . . at least, not about your intelligence."

I'm surprised at her apology. I didn't think those words would ever pass her lips, if I'm honest. Though she didn't apologize for thinking I'm some groupie-fucking manwhore. But that didn't hurt nearly as much her thinking I'm stupid. I tilt her chin up, meeting her eyes again. "Apology accepted. I'm sorry for being late. Won't happen again."

She nods. "Good. Okay then, tomorrow at five. For real this time?" She grabs her bag from the table, tossing it over her shoulder like she's leaving.

"Fuck that. We're getting started tonight," I say, my hard tone not allowing any argument. Except from her, apparently.

She smirks, tossing her red hair back over shoulder. "Sorry, I've got plans."

I want to shut her smart mouth up with a kiss. Or maybe a kiss to my dick. Either might be acceptable and would stick with her apparent rule about not fucking.

Too bad because I think some combo sex-study sessions would be a rather great motivator to get my grades up.

Instead, I take her elbow firmly but gently enough that she could pull away if she wanted to. I guide her deeper into the library toward a shadowed corner far away from the main entrance where people constantly come and go. Vaguely, I wonder if anyone has seen our exchange and wondered what was going on. Shit.

"Come on, Brat," I growl over my shoulder at her. "We've got studying to do."

Once in the relative safety of the private corner, without a soul in sight, I push her back against the wall, crowding in front of her. She sputters, eyes wide. "What the hell, Zach? You can't just drag me around like some bastard, big-dicked jock who thinks people should bow at his feet and live life according to your timetable." She's ranting again, her voice getting a bit loud for the library.

I press into her, letting her feel me and silencing her with my rumbled, "Bastard? Big-dicked? Sounds like you'd like to know for sure. Say the word, and I'll pull it out for you, Norma." I know she can feel that I'm already half-hard just from being this close to her, but the thought of her asking to see my cock has a rush of blood going south. I wait a beat to see if by some stroke of God's grace, she does. When she stays silent, giving me a death glare, I continue. "Look, I apologized for being late, but we really do need to get started. I have a paper due in two days, and as much as I hate to admit it, I do need your help. I need at least a B-minus on this paper." I lay on a bit of the puppy dog eye treatment, hoping she gives in. My future lies in her hands.

CHAPTER 3

*M*y heart and my head both pound furiously as Zach pulls me into one of the back corners of the library. I don't know why I'm following him without protest. I should be kicking him in the balls for laying his hands on me. His big, rough, warm hands touching the skin of my arm . . . I wonder what those hands would feel like on more sensitive parts, like my belly, my ass, my pussy.

I shake my head. No, that's so not what is happening here. It can't be. Because I am *not* turned on by his charming caveman act. Still, when we stop, I'm dimly aware that it's the romance section, of all places.

Fighting my own attraction, I take it out on him, whisper-yelling as he presses me against the wall. "What the hell, Zach?" There's more to my rant, though I'm mindlessly insulting him now. My breath is gone, no oxygen to fuel my brain as my body tunes in on the electricity arcing between us.

Then he leans against me, fire sparking as the connection between our bodies completes. I curse the separation of our clothing and then realize he's offering to pull his dick out right here in the library. I'm shocked into silence, though a part of my brain begs for me to say yes, to have him do that, right here, right now. I can feel his hard thickness against my belly, something that should have me fighting back with sharp words.

Instead, I'm fumbling for something to say like some useless airhead. Pushed up against him, it's like every cell in my body has come to life with an itch that's both maddening and wonderful. Hazily, I wonder if this is what most people feel when they lust after someone. No one has ever stood up to my personality long enough for me to even really consider them the way I'm currently considering Zach.

And I'm definitely considering him. Six feet four, I'd bet, with wide shoulders and muscles that ride that fine line between bulging and lean, wearing a team T-shirt that makes me want to pull it over his head for a better view. His hair is still damp a bit, because of the shower he was late for, but the darkness added to his shaggy blond hair makes him look more carefree. His blue eyes are diving into my soul, and the flash of his smile, teeth so white he could star in a toothpaste commercial, brings me back to reality.

This can't happen. Not him. Not me. Not here. Not now. Not. Ever.

The thought brings a hint of sadness with it, and it's mirrored by the imploring look he's giving me. Luckily, part of my brain was paying attention to his words, and

I'm able to give a reasonable answer even though most of my body is ready to roll over and purr for him.

What the hell, Norma?

"Fine. Two days for a paper isn't much time to work with, so let's get started," I finally answer, hating that I'm giving in but not ready to leave him either.

His expression instantly changes to a smirk at the victory. "Great. Do you need to text anyone to cancel your plans?"

He knows I was bluffing. I don't have plans and definitely don't have a date. It was the principle of the matter. "No, asshole. I don't need to text anyone." I plop onto the couch in this corner, letting my bag fall gently to the floor.

Zach sits down beside me, leaving a space between us. "I knew it, Brat. You were just trying to get a rise out of me, weren't you?" I shrug, not willing to confirm or deny his assessment.

I fight a smile. "I get it now. My boss told me 'good luck' with this whole mess, and in hindsight, I'm thinking that means she knows what a cocky jerk you are. Maybe you know her. She seems to follow football a bit. Erica Waters?" Though I'm teasing, I desperately want him to say he hasn't slept with her. I don't know why that would seem too close to home, but it does.

But he shakes his head. "Nope, don't know her. I also don't *know* her. But I do really want you to say that again." He winks like I should know what he's talking about, and then it hits me.

25

I look him full in the eye, intentionally adding emphasis as I breathily say in my best porn star imitation, "Caaahhck–y jerk." His eyes watch the word leave my lips and then jump to mine, full of humor.

"Oh, you think you're funny, Brat? Turnaround is fair play," he says brazenly. He grabs a book from the shelf in front of us, not bothering to read the cover, but I can see that it's titled *Hot For The Billionaire*. I roll my eyes until he opens the book and starts actually reading.

"I'm going to fuck you raw and rough, rip that little pussy to shreds with my big cock." He changes his voice to a falsetto. *"Yes, John, screw me with that big cock. I'm your slut and I want you inside me so badly. I gaze upon his flawless magnificence with unbridled need, my glistening sugar walls begging for the massive manhood inside his slacks."*

I grab at the book, trying to get it from his hands. "Stop it!" I beg, trying not to laugh and pissed off at the little giggle that escapes my mouth. I don't know what's more disturbing, his reading this or that I'm actually getting turned on by his saying such over-the-top cheesy, dirty things in that silly voice. "You're making an ass of yourself!"

Zach chuckles, tossing the book back on the shelf. "Do women actually read that shit? But I guess you seem to have enjoyed it. That little giggle was cute."

I roll my eyes, snarling. "Get over yourself. You're *totally* not funny." Except my snarl sounds more like a purr. A hungry, ravenous purr.

"Really? I think I see your breath quickening." His eyes

drop to my chest, and I force myself not to arch my back and show off for him.

"Get your eyes checked," I sass. "You might be blind." The jab is weak at best, but it's all I have in this moment.

"Saw that passage perfectly fine. And I shut that cute little mouth of yours."

I think my cheeks are turning as red as my hair.

C'mon, Norma, he probably drops lines like that with all the girls. And this is not real.

"You didn't shut anything," I growl, but sheesh, the growl makes it sound like a dare.

He hears it too, his grin growing wider, cockier, as if he knows what his playful alpha attitude is doing to me. "Come on, you're all attitude and a big mouth, but you're not that bad. And you're enjoying this, just like I am."

I need to get out of here before I transform into some weak, mewling kitten lapping at his feet. Puffing out my chest, I gather myself up. "Truth? You're *maybe* not so bad. But we do need to work. Two days, remember?"

The light, teasing mood that had surrounded us evaporates and I'm sorry I said anything. But it's the reality of what's going on between us. He may be fun to spar with, and he might enjoy getting under my skin, but at the end of the day, this is about one thing only—his grades.

He sighs. "Yeah, two days. Let's get to work."

Neither of us seem particularly driven to study, but he

pulls out his copy of *Paradise Lost* and a spiral filled with more chicken scratches than notes. I glance through it, trying to gauge where he's at in the story and what level of comprehension he's getting from the old poem that's decidedly complex. But the more I try to read through his notes, the less I know where he's at. "Okay, how about this. Explain what you've gotten from the story so far and what the assignment is supposed to include."

His eyes go wide and then roll. "Fuck if I know. Something about idols and God not wanting churches?"

I hum. "Uhm, okay, not exactly, but that gets a start on what to focus on for this paper, at least."

He sighs in relief. "Thanks, Norma. I appreciate your help."

It sounds real, maybe the first totally real thing he's said to me since he walked up on me bitching about him. No game, no agenda, no teasing, just honestly grateful for the assistance.

We spend the next hour going through Spark Notes and his professor's PowerPoint presentation about the poem, making some good headway in Zach's understanding and writing the outline for his paper. He's doing better than I would've expected, considering the intricacies of this piece. Surprisingly, without the snark and bites, we make a pretty good team as we work our way through the story.

When he answers a particularly complex question correctly, he celebrates by scooting closer and throwing his hand up for a high-five.

I laughingly smack his palm with mine. "Good job. Now, what about Eve?" Though I'm continuing my lesson with him, it's on auto-pilot as my brain focuses on the length of his thigh touching mine, his hip next to my hip. I remind myself, *grades, tutoring, fake relationship, nothing more.*

But his voice is huskier, too, as he speaks. "She's temptation." He moves his finger to my thigh, just the one fingertip tracing through the denim of my jeans. "Fiery temptation that leads Adam astray," he says, and I don't think we're analyzing literature anymore. His touch gets higher, the brush of the back of his hand a breath away from the heat of my center. It's all I can do not to buck my hips to get that contact.

I take a steadying breath. "But before she was Adam's temptation, Eve was tempted herself by the snake." The words are filthier than I intended them to be, but when Zach leans in close to whisper hotly in my ear, I don't regret them.

"And are you, Norma? Are you tempted?" he growls.

My mind is saying *run.* My body is saying *don't move a muscle.* "You're incorrigible," I finally relent, trying to fight the tidal wave of desire rolling up from my stomach as I sag against the couch, tilting my hips ever so slightly closer to his hand.

"Oh, yeah?" he asks, leaning against my side a bit harder, trapping me between him and the arm of the couch. His full lips are barely an inch away from my ear and his words send warm tingles down my body. "Well, you're not moving, and I think you're a smart-mouthed little brat who needs to be taught a thing or two about temptation and what happens when you tempt a cocky bastard like me.''

I'm shocked at the way he's talking to me. I should smack him, or at the very least stand up and stomp my way right out of the library. But I'm frozen. I'm turned on. I'm putty in his hands, and he fucking knows it.

Hell, maybe I am just as weak as those groupies. But I can understand it when he's playing me like a fucking violin.

Good God, I want him to take me, right here and right now. It's a scary thought. I never thought I'd find someone to challenge my mouthiness, and I certainly never considered it'd be with some football player jock type. But even if he wasn't a decent verbal sparring partner, which he shockingly is, he's doing something to my body I've never experienced. And it's real, so very fucking real.

And I want it. I want more. Who cares if that makes me weak? Right now, sure as fuck not me.

"You think you could teach me?" If I'd said it sweetly, he'd have probably smiled. As it is, I say it with disdain, like I somehow doubt his abilities. To be clear, I don't, but I'm not going to let him in on that little fact just yet.

His smirk flashes and I hear the unspoken 'challenge accepted.' "Yeah, Norma, I think I could teach you all sorts of things about temptation. You think I don't know how badly you want me to bend you over this couch and fill you full of cock? You're tempted to let me, and better yet, I'm tempted to do it.''

His fingers flatten against my center, stopping my argument as he grinds against me. My breath hitches, and he keeps talking. "I want to hear your bratty mouth moaning my name against my palm because I have to muffle your cries so no one hears us."

I whimper weakly, offering the barest of objections. "We shouldn't. You should stop."

"But you're practically begging me not to stop," he says, his fingers moving faster, and even through the fabric separating us, I know he can feel how hot and wet I am. "This is what you want, isn't it?" I can't deny the truth.

It's torture. I want to say no just to show him that I'm stronger than he is. But my lips won't form the word. Instead, I clutch at his iron-hard arm, gasping and on the edge of coming.

"Yes." The word comes out without permission and he knows it.

Zach pulls away, leaving me weak as my body screams for release. "What? Keep going," I groan.

He looks at me expectantly, waiting for me to realize that he's not going to give in. "Fucking bastard," I say, sitting up straight on the couch from where I'd slouched into his touch.

The corners of his mouth lift in amusement, but he reaches down and adjusts himself in his jeans. He looks huge and hard, and uncomfortably contained in their confines, as affected by this whole thing as I am. Even though I'm furious, there's a horny bitch inside me that begs him to unzip and let *his* snake free. "Every day, after practice, we can meet. Five is too early. Eight would be better. I won't be late."

"What makes you think—" I gasp, my body still crying out. I shut up, realizing that my protests sound hollow even to my own ears. They must sound pathetic to him. "Fuck you," I sneer. I might be so horny I can't see straight, but I've still got some pride.

But Zach smiles that panty-melting grin, leaning in to tease me one last time. "Keep saying that and maybe you'll get to. Honestly, I'm really hoping you do."

He stands up and adjusts himself once more, knowing that my eyes will follow the movement. "See you tomorrow, Brat. It's a date."

I watch him walk away, glaring holes in his back. Inside, I want to scream and call him a bastard who doesn't deserve to touch me, much less deserve my help. But deeper inside, I know I'm going to be here tomorrow at eight. On the dot.

CHAPTER 4

NORMA

*D*ear Diary,

Remember when I said I'd wear my virgin badge proudly? Wait until I found someone worthy enough, that lit not just my body aflame, but my mind too?

I fucking found him.

In the worst package ever. Oh, it's a pretty package, for sure, but I always figured I'd be repulsed by his "type", the cocky jock. But something about him set me on fire in a way I'd never known.

I spent the night replaying his dirty words, my fingers replacing his remembered ones. I didn't stop like he did though. I'm pretty sure my loud neighbor thinks I had a guy over because I damn sure said his name when I came.

But this morning, in the light of day, I'm humiliated that an assignment that should be relatively straightforward has turned into something so foundationally stupid. I know better than to think a guy is going to hang with me through my . . . brattiness. I've never actually been called a brat, and in fact, I rather take offense to it since I know the 'spoiled rich girl' assumptions people make when they find out my last name. But when Zach called me that, it almost sounded like he appreciated my mouthiness, like he was daring me to say more, anticipating what smart remark I'd come up with next.

But a guy like him? He's not a forever type, barely a fuck-em-and-leave-em type, and then there's this whole blade hanging over my head that is our fake relationship. Definitely not who my body should be responding to, not who I should want to spar with, not who I should be thinking about in anything other than a profes-sional tutoring way.

Fuck. I wish he would just show up tonight and let me tutor him, start over, and forget yesterday ever happened.

Fat chance of that though.

Because if I can't forget, he probably can't either.

No matter how hard I try, I haven't been able to get Zach out of my mind. What else do you call it when you sit through two morning classes and don't remember a damn thing about either of them? Hell, I'm not even sure if I sat in the right rooms today. I might have been in another class and not even noticed. Now I've got work at *The Chronicle* to do, and I'm still not sure what the fuck is going on.

I try to keep my head down and my focus sharp, but I'm broken out of my reverie when Erica interrupts. "Hey, how did your tutoring session go?" I'm in the editing office because I can't imagine being out in the main room right now, supposedly working on a column about unprotected sex on campus. Sometimes, when the universe wants to send you a message, it whispers. Right now though, it's screaming at me with blinking neon LED lights.

I check my screen, looking at the last thing I typed. *Sex*, of course. Great, I've been at a complete standstill for the last ten minutes. Talk about something screaming at me. My cursor's doing it with its incessant blinking, and I'm spacing out because of it.

I quickly minimize my window and look up, formulating my response. Do I tell her what an ass Zach started off as? Or what about how he was still walking that line as he drove me wild in a totally different way before walking away as I asked him to make me come? Or about how I want him to fuck me every which way from Sunday and handle me like he handles a football? Fast and hard, with that light touch that makes sure he scores constantly?

"I . . . uh . . . it was productive," I finally lie, a flush coming to my cheeks. "We covered a few basic rules. That kinda stuff. Didn't get too deep into Milton, but you know how it is."

Erica quirks an eyebrow. "*That kinda stuff*? What is that kind of stuff?"

I don't how to reply to Erica, mainly because I know we covered jack and shit. "Uh, you know, he was late, so we only had time to cover schedules and ground rules. Stuff like that. But he has a paper due tomorrow. We did the outline last night, and he'll write it tonight so it's ready to go. A good grade there should help his overall grade quite a bit."

It's the truth but barely touches the surface of the whole truth. It seems to satisfy Erica though. "Thank goodness. I was scared he'd no-show on you, but Coach Jefferson said he really stressed how important this is to Zach. Was he okay with the tutoring, at least?"

I look at her incredulously. "Seriously? You thought he'd get forced into tutoring, begrudgingly show up late, and then be happy as a lark to admit to needing help? No, he wasn't okay. He was a cocky bastard who fought me tooth and nail at every turn to establish dominance. Honestly, he's an arrogant son of a bitch who thinks he's God's gift to women." I realize that I'm painting an accurate, albeit not very savory, image of Zach and belatedly try to temper my harsh words. "But once we sat down and got to work, it was fine."

Erica cringes at my assault of Zach's character. "I'm so sorry, Norma. But can you stick with it? It'd be good for both of you, I think. Him, because he needs someone strong enough to bust his balls and make him work. You, because the athletic department will owe you. I'm sure you could parlay this into a one-on-one interview with the star quarterback, and maybe the head coach too, after we win the conference championship."

Sports reporting, also known as the sweat sock circuit, isn't my dream gig. But a featured interview with Zach and Coach Jefferson would be a dream come true assignment for most, definitely a byline highlight for my portfolio.

I nod. "Of course. Like I said, we already made plans to meet tonight. I knew this would be a hard assignment, but I can handle it." I hope that speaking the words will put it out in the universe to make it true because while I know I can keep my mouth shut and I can be a stellar tutor, I seriously doubt my ability to handle Zach in any real way. He's got me in the palm of his hand. Or he did last night . . . literally.

CUTTING MY TIME SHORT AT THE NEWSPAPER, I RUN BACK to my apartment to change clothes. I need something conservative, something that will armor me against Zach's attack.

First to go is my slim-fitting tank top which is just a school spirit shirt, but it does hug what boobs I have pretty well, and I want Zach's attention focused on learning, not my assets. I switch out my pretty bra for a sturdy, plain one and then pull on a loose-fitting graphic T-shirt from the mall. I knot it tightly at my waist, knowing that it won't let a roving hand wander underneath. I ditch my jeans in favor of a long, black maxi skirt and boots that have the smallest heel because at five foot four, I don't own anything without *some* sort of heel except for gym shoes.

Last but not least, I pull my hair up in a messy bun and wrap a folded scarf around my head, letting the tails of the knot stand out. I slip my glasses on, even though I usually only need them for prolonged computer work, and then look in the mirror.

I look like an urban hippie and a librarian combined their closets and I pulled everything I'm wearing, head to toe, from the crazy mismatch. It's perfect. If nothing else, any curves I have are hidden and it'll take Zach longer to get his hands on my skin.

And that's the problem, because if he does, I'm in trouble. Every time he looked at me last night, I felt like I was about to catch fire. Even now, thinking about what he did to me, it's making my pulse pound and my heart speed like a drag racer.

I sag against the dresser, my breathing ragged, my body once again flooded with powerful hormones. Jesus. What the fuck is happening to me? I glare at myself in the mirror, talking aloud. "Okay, Norma Jean Blackstone. Get your shit together and be the ball buster you always are. It's just a tutoring session, and he's just a regular guy. Nothing is going to happen except studying. You got it?" I point at the mirror, threatening my reflection and hoping the warning sticks when I'm alone with Zach.

With a sigh and two sets of crossed fingers, I grab my bag and head over to the library. It's early, but I have plenty of work of my own to do, especially since I'll be spending the bulk of the evening with Zach's paper on Milton. Sure, I could study at home. It's probably even quieter and has fewer distractions, but getting there will hopefully make eight o'clock come sooner rather than later.

But as I settle in at a table on the first floor, I know I misjudged. I'm not getting shit done because I keep glancing up every time the doors open. I see people come and go, none of them Zach because he's not supposed to be here for almost two hours.

Eventually, I do find my groove and get some work done while I wait.

CHAPTER 5

ZACH

Knowing I'm going to see Norma tonight is putting a little extra pep in my step all day, and folks have noticed. "Jesus, try not to dislocate my wrist next time?" Lenny Smalls, one of my team-mates, says as he tosses the ball back to me lightly. We're running 'card routes', just working our grooves for later, and he's shaking out his left hand. "It was just a ten-yard route, Zach."

His whining rolls right off my back. "Just feeling it today, man. You need to put some extra padding on your pussy or something?" I ask, teasing him but barely thinking about Lenny.

Since our encounter last night, my thoughts have been filled with Norma, the way the sassy minx looked as she melted for me, but also how she wasn't putting up with my shit. I was right. A soft Norma was a sight to behold, but I liked the sassy one too.

I can't imagine dealing with that smart mouth of hers for another tutoring session without giving her the pounding we both want. Hell, maybe she can use that as an incentive to get me to study harder. The dirty thought makes me smirk, and then I reconsider. Maybe I can use dick to get her to help me. I have a feeling she's gonna be the one dragging me around by the balls more than the reverse.

Coach calls the next play and I grin. My passes have had enough zip that I'm sending frozen ropes to my receivers, Lenny included. But this one is all me, an old high school play we keep just for shits and giggles. I take the snap from the shotgun and immediately pitch the ball to our starting running back, Marcus. The defense doesn't know if it's a run or a pass, and in that confusion, I take off upfield.

I'm all alone when Marcus stops and throws the ball across the field in a decent pass. I have to slow down to catch it, but the change in speed allows me to juke the strong safety right out of his cleats as I fake him out and run the ball in.

Sure, it's just practice, but the offense is grinning when I get back, and the defense can't say a fucking thing. They just got torched and they damn well know it, even if they don't want to lay any big hits on us.

"Hey, Zach, don't forget it's only practice," Coach Buckley, our QB coach and offensive coordinator, says to me as I rejoin the sidelines and my backup, Jake 'Snake' Robertson, gets a few plays in. "They'll be trying to take your head off if you keep showboating, and we need you 100% come Saturday."

"Maybe . . . but they won't be able to even if they try," I reply. "And I'm gonna own Eastern's ass like my name's tattooed there."

"You're feeling your oats more than usual," Coach says. "What's going on? I'm digging the beast mode today."

"Thanks," I reply. Coach Buckley is young for such a high-level position, only twenty-seven, so he's a lot like a big brother to me and not just a coach. "Just wait until Saturday."

I rotate back in, and no matter who the defense puts in, I'm lighting it up. It's like a damn game of Madden, and finally, Coach blows his whistle. "That's enough! I keep you out here any longer, and I'm going to have to check the defense for their balls."

The offense is in high spirits, and even the defense feels some confidence as we congratulate each other. They know we're going to kick ass Saturday, and that's the important thing.

Only one person seems to be in a pissy mood. "I could've done it better," Jake says petulantly as we do our cooldown stretches. "All that dancing bullshit is fine for practice, but it's not gonna work in the game. They were taking it easy on him out there."

I glance over at Jake, a little pissed. "You had reps with the offense today too, remember? Did those not count either? You want more time? Earn it."

"That's enough," Coach Buckley says, but I've already dismissed Jake. Instead, my mind is on Norma Jean, who's going to be waiting for me once I shower up and get changed. I let her go yesterday, but today won't be so easy. I've had all night and day to think of what I want to do to her.

"Hey, Knight," Coach Jefferson, our head coach, says after I shower and leave the locker room. He's old-school, with white hair and a belly that sticks out in his polo shirt, and he runs summer practice like we're trying out for the Marines. But he knows football and has put four QBs in the pros. Best of all, he'll give as much to you as you give to him. I couldn't ask for a better guide to the League. "Looked good out there."

"What can I say, Coach?" I reply with a grin. "I play to win. They won't fucking know what hit 'em Saturday."

He laughs. "That's the spirit! But let me talk to you for a moment. My office."

I step into his office and take a seat. "What's up, Coach?"

He settles in, grabbing an antacid out of the big bowl of them he keeps next to his computer. Maybe it's the eighteen-hour work days, but he munches Tums like candy, and as he gives me a look, I figure I'm the cause of this particular munch. "I got a call from Erica Waters this morning. Listen, no bullshit with the tutoring, alright? She said you were late and gave the tutor a hard time. I don't want you sidelined because you can't act like an adult. This is a big ask of that girl. Don't fuck it up, Son."

I shift around, pissed that Norma tattled on me to her boss. But then again, she probably got called into a sit-down just like this. "Coach, I'm taking the tutoring seriously, going to get my grades up so I maintain eligibility. No worries. And I might've pushed the line on the tutor a little, but . . . well, you know."

He nods. "Yeah, I know how you boys are. I was a football hotshot once too." He pats his belly like he can't believe what's happened to him since his college ball days. "But listen very carefully on this one. Don't mix business and pleasure. And that tutor, she's business even if we've got some shitty dating lie in place for cover. If you want to fool around with someone, go for it, but not her, and not until we get this grade stuff handled."

"Coach, she's cute, and it wouldn't interfere with my—"

"Stow it. I've heard that a thousand times. Don't do anything to mess up your future because you've got a fucking bright one, Son. A golden ticket . . . if you can get your grades up. She's got your grades by the balls because you need her. Don't hand her your literal ones too. Business and pleasure, Zachary, do not mix." His words are delivered with the wisdom of a man who's seen too many guys screw something up, and I take them seriously.

I nod. "Yes sir." He nods back, dismissing me, and I make a run for it before I run his blood pressure up any higher.

I leave the football complex and head toward the library. As I walk, I stew over Coach's words. Is he right? Should I leave Norma solidly in the business category and let what happened last night be a one-time thing, just letting this dating shit settle in the background in case someone asks? Or can I tempt fate and do a bit of mixing of business and pleasure?

I think of the way Norma tempted me last night and I know the answer.

I'M JOGGING MY WAY UP THE STEPS TO THE LIBRARY AT five minutes to eight, feeling good in a fresh pair of jeans and a team T-shirt. Pausing at the door, I do a quick run-through of my hair with my hands. I normally don't give a shit about what my hair looks like after practice, content to let it do whatever the fuck it wants. But I feel like upping my game for some reason.

After all, little Norma seems to have a way of finding chinks in my armor and stabbing me in them. And that's not going to continue to be the damn case. Entering the library, I look around, finding the little alcove where I first saw her. I'm already thinking of it as 'our spot' . . . except she's not there.

"Hmm," I mutter, turning around and checking but seeing nobody. "Little Miss Perfect gives me shit about being late and then she doesn't show up?"

But then I scan again, and I spot her off in a far corner but with a direct sightline to the front door. She's lost in her work, her foot tapping under the table to whatever music is pumping through her earbuds and her eyes flicking from the book on the table to the computer screen in front of her.

She looks sweet like this, without the fire she shoots when she looks at me. I approach slowly, not wanting to break the spell she's under. As I get closer, I take the opportunity to look her up and down. A smirk takes my face when I realize how she's dressed, like an oddly naughty librarian. It's nothing like her outfit from yesterday but still so cute that my cock twitches in my jeans.

I set my bag on the table, and she jumps, yanking her earbuds out. "Fuck, you scared me," she scolds.

I point to my watch. "Just making sure you noted that I'm right on time. You look nice." I smirk, waiting for her sarcastic bite back.

"What?" she asks, playing innocent. "You don't like my clothes?"

I snort, shaking my head. I lean in close, one arm on either side of her to whisper in her ear. "You can try all you want to cover up, but we both know the truth. You got all dressed up like that because you needed a few more layers of cloth armor between me and your sweet little pussy because you're afraid your body is going to betray you again. But you've got a bad girl side, and we're going to explore it sooner rather than later. I'm looking forward to seeing you accept that fact. I think it'll be . . . beautiful. Speaking of beautiful, right now, I'm thinking of flipping that long skirt up and making you hold it so I can grab a couple of handfuls of your ass and get at your pussy from behind."

I stay silent, letting that imagery fill her mind as I watch the flush cover her freckled face. And when I see that pink tinge to her cheeks, I say a silent apology to Coach Jefferson. He's done so much for me, but I can't honor his request this time. Because that hint of blush just gave me as much satisfaction as a pass perfectly thrown for a game-winning touchdown, and I've barely started with Norma.

"You can't say things like that to me!" she argues half-heartedly, turning slightly to look up at me from inside the cage of my arms.

It sounds like she got the business and pleasure talk too, or at least one similar to it. But yeah, I'm mixing that shit up.

She's practically trembling as I capture her with my gaze, a wolf ready to stare into the eyes of its prey before taking it down. It's like she's trying her hardest to resist, but all it will take is one simple push, one touch, to send her over the brink.

I chance a glance to her lips, beseeching them. "Admit it. You liked it, didn't you? No shame in that. Don't be shy."

Her hand trembles on the tabletop, so I reach up and cover it with my own. She doesn't resist as I rub soothing circles along the back of it and trace her fingers, marveling at how soft they are. "Zach . . ."

"It's our little secret," I whisper as I put her hand on my thigh, sliding it up with no resistance until it comes to rest on the hard bulge between my legs. It's honest, and I'm not faking a thing as I look into those pretty eyes. "Truth be told, I haven't been able to think about anything else either. You're sexy as fuck, Norma . . . and

I'm not all bad. I can be more than an asshole if you're willing to give me a chance. So tell me the truth. Tell me you liked it."

"I loved it," she whispers, her hand tightening almost without even thinking. "God, I loved it."

*M*y hand rests where it is, but suddenly, I realize where we are, what I'm doing, and who I'm doing it with. What the hell am I thinking?

"No!" I protest, jerking my hand away from the big bulge between his legs and trying to take back my words. "You're playing with my head. I didn't mean that!"

Zach grins, not letting go of my hand as he stands up, shoving my stuff in my bag and tossing it over his shoulder. He leads me deeper into the library. My feet don't even attempt to stop him, following him willingly as we hike the steps to the fourth floor and then twist and turn until we're in a darkened section. It's musty up here, like nobody's been around this section in a long time.

"Zach," I try to protest, even as my feet follow him. "We can't do this." I'm not sure if I'm trying to convince him or me. But he finds a secluded table and pulls a chair out for me like a gentleman. The gesture is unexpectedly civil, and I smile as I sit.

He sits beside me after turning his chair slightly so that it faces me. "Ok, Brat. Hit me with them."

I'm confused and my eyebrows pull together. "Hit you with what?"

"Your reasons why not. I'll go first. We're going to be spending time together, getting to know each other, and people already think we're dating or they soon will, and we have chemistry, even when we're smack talking at each other. Why not add a little reality to the pretend? No harm, no foul, just fun."

I can't help but laugh. "Those are your reasons why not?"

He chuckles. "No, you take one side of the argument, and I'll take the other. That's how debate works, or have you not learned that? I thought you were supposed to be a smarty pants?"

The tease is silly, but it works, making the moment lighter. "I *am* a smarty pants, but more importantly, I'm a smart ass. So there's reason one why not. It's fun to jab with you, but that won't last. You're going to get tired of my always pushing your buttons. Everyone does. And I'm not sure I'm ready for your level of *casual* fun. It's a bit of a bigger deal to me. I think your way sounds . . . dangerous."

He rubs at his chin like he's contemplating my arguments, but I can see the light in his eyes. "Agree to disagree. I find your button pushing endearing in an odd way. Can't say I can explain it, but it's true. And you say dangerous like it's a bad thing, but what I'm hearing is that you might enjoy a little danger. Fuck knows, I would. And you seem rather risky to me too, Brat." His voice is full of promise, the hazards seeming fewer than the possibilities when he says it like that.

I smile at the idea that of the two of us, I could be the dangerous one. Ridiculous. "Okay. Agree to disagree. But what I think we can both agree on is that you have a paper to write tonight and we should get to work."

He grumbles, muttering something about 'this conversation not being over', but he pulls out his laptop and book. "Okay, now what?"

I sigh. "Now, you write. Here's the outline we worked on last night. Use it to do the opening paragraph and then we'll reread it to clean it up."

His nod is reluctant, but he gets to work, his fingers deftly flying cross the keys as he writes. A mere fifteen minutes later, he sits back in his chair. "Done."

He turns his laptop toward me and I begin to read his introductory paragraph. It's good, better than I would've expected if I'm honest, though my harshly judgmental thoughts embarrass me a bit. "Good job. Next paragraph is based on this quote . . ." I point to the one in his notes.

But he doesn't get to work. Instead, he smirks at me knowingly. "You thought it'd suck, didn't you? That a dumb jock like me wouldn't be able to write for shit. But I'll let you in on a little secret. I aced English in high school and can actually string together a sentence, using commas and everything. This professor and me just don't click, and I particularly hate *Paradise Lost*."

I blush, the truth a bit of a jagged dig, but probably no more so than my expectation of him. "Honestly, yeah. Sorry for the preconceived idea. Stereotypes aren't always true. Hell, they're *usually* not true."

"Apology not accepted this time, Brat. Gonna take more than that," he says, reaching forward to wrap a tendril of my hair around his finger. It feels intimate with the rest of my hair piled on top of my head, like his finger is *this close* to brushing against the silky skin of my neck.

"Zach, what are you doing? What are you talking about? We agreed—" I say, but my voice is quiet.

"*You* decided. I didn't agree to shit. I just blasted one of your judgments about me. Tell me something that'll change one of mine about you."

I think he's trying to stall on his work, but he seems genuinely interested. I quickly rack my brain for some-thing, then offer, "People think I'm spoiled sometimes, like I get everything handed to me because of my dad. But that's not true. He's more of the 'work hard and earn it' camp than the 'want my kids to have it better than I did' group. He does pay for some things, my tuition and my apartment, and I know that's a *huge* benefit lots of people don't get. But it comes with strings, and we butt heads sometimes when he expects me to give in to what he wants. He raised me to be a leader, a fighter, but then he wants me to fall in line like one of his underlings at work." It's a big share for me, and a rarely-voiced criticism of my dad. He's a good man and a good father, but no one is perfect.

Needing to get back on more solid ground, I flip the

switch and let my armor pop back into place. "So, that's me . . . poor little rich girl." Zach eyes me thoughtfully, like he can see right through my shield, so I try to distract him. "So if it's not *Paradise Lost*, what is your favorite book?"

He leans close, whispering in my ear, "Right now, I'm thinking my favorite book is the *Kama Sutra* because whatever is on page sixty-nine, I'm game for it." He sits back, smirking. I know I walked right into that, but it almost feels like he's directing us back to lighter, looser, sexier conversation because he knew I was uncomfortable with what I shared. Like his dirty joke was actually to be nice to me.

So I respond as expected, playing along, "Ugh, disgusting. Is that all you think about? Your brain is going to need a transfusion if the blood stays in your *other* head all the time."

He chuckles and grabs at his crotch like he's checking for blood flow, then knocks on the side of his temple. "Nope, I think we've got an appropriate division of blood supply. A little going north, a little going south."

We both laugh, and then I tap on his outline, signaling that we should get back to work.

And that's how each segment of his paper goes. He works, I read over it, and we pause for conversations. Somehow, through the evening, I feel like I get to know him a bit better.

He's not quite the cocky bastard jock I thought, though there's a heavy dose of that on the surface. But beneath, he's actually a nice guy, albeit one with a wicked tongue that he uses to lash at me deliciously, both literally and figuratively.

His barbed banter is exciting, making me anticipate what zinger he's going to lob my way next. He sometimes goes for the lowest common denominator joke, usually sexual, but then he'll turn right around and surprise me with something a bit more high-brow. I swear there was even a comment about *The Great Gatsby* but I'm going to need to check my quote source to be sure. Of course, I didn't let him know that.

But he's also used that sinful tongue to drive me crazy in a much more literal way. Around paragraph eight, he slipped his hand around the back of my neck, pulling me toward him as I read, to lay little licking kisses along my skin. The only skin I left exposed, I think, recognizing the irony in that.

By paragraph twenty, he whispered dirty promises in my ear as he slipped my skirt up my thighs to get at my hot pussy. I'd protested for a second, more out of some feeling that I should than because I actually wanted to. I'd been desperately close to coming again, but he'd recognized that I'd finished reading the paragraph and stopped, going back to work on the next section. I'd growled and told him not to start games he couldn't finish. But he'd just grinned evilly and said that he planned on finishing . . . the paper *and* me.

It's almost eleven when he finally finishes his essay, clicking *Submit Online* to turn the completed assignment in. I look around and realize the library has cleared out, though our secluded corner has been pretty quiet all night. I find that

I don't want the night to end. The tutoring has been fun, almost like a team effort to get his paper done by the deadline. But more importantly, it has been fun to spend time with Zach, and he's got me on edge from all his touches and dirty whispers. Hell, I never knew having to be quiet in the library could be so damn sexy.

But I'm not sure what he's thinking. Has this just been fun and games to pass the time while he got his work done? Hell, for all I know, he's off to some party full of sorority girls and cheerleaders, and I'm going to go home to get myself off to thoughts of him. Again. Even though I know I shouldn't.

"So, now what?" I ask, adding a bit of sass to my tone and lifting one eyebrow, hoping he hears the challenge and takes me up on it but knowing that if he doesn't, I'll have my answer right there.

He smirks. "I told you, Brat. I was gonna finish my paper and then finish . . . you."

I should say no. I know that I should not do this. It's epically stupid in so many ways. But Zach checks all the boxes on my checklist, both good and bad. Football player, cocky jock, bastard asshole, kind, funny, quick-witted, sharp-tongued . . . Zach.

And I know I'm going to give in. But I won't do it easily. That's not who I am.

"You think you can? Hmm, I don't know. Guys sometimes have a hard time closing the deal. I could probably tutor you there if you want," I say, letting false doubt fill my voice. I have no qualms that Zach could probably get me off in minutes, especially considering the way he's been building me up all night.

He leans in and kisses me full on the lips. It's fierce and hard, communicating in no uncertain terms that he's ready to meet this challenge. My inner bitch jumps for joy, clapping with excitement.

He pulls back, both of us panting, and then he gives me that arrogant smirk. "I don't need a damn bit of tutoring for this, Brat."

He gets up, and I'm confused for a second at where he's going. But with a quick look around, he drops to his knees and crawls under the table. He grasps my knees and forces them wide, sitting on the floor between them. And then he flips my skirt up to my lap. Damn maxi skirt that was supposed to protect me from this, but right now, I'm thanking God that it's making my pussy easy-access for whatever Zach is about to do.

He grabs my inner thighs, kneading them in his rough grip as he inhales me. "Fuck, Norma, dressing like a good girl but wearing sexy Victoria's Secret panties like a bad girl," his voice rumbles, so close to where I want him, the heat of his breath good, but I tilt toward him, looking for more.

"This is such a bad idea. We're going to get caught . . ." I murmur, but my brain is already shutting down all the solid arguments for why I should definitely not be doing this. Not here, but most of all, not with Zach. This has danger written all over it, for my body, my heart, and my career. Almost like he can hear me but interprets the same situation differently, Zach smiles ferally against my thigh.

"We won't get caught if you're quiet, Norma. Think you can be quiet while I eat your sweet little pussy? Or maybe you like that someone might catch us, might watch me fuck your cunt with my tongue? That little bit of danger get you off?" He emphasizes each question with a stroke of his thumb against my clit, but it's through the silk of my panties . . . good but not enough.

I whimper, biting my lip to try to stay quiet.

"Say yes or I'll stop. I want to hear you give in, knowing that you're choosing this." Zach's voice is a hushed growl.

Needing to fight him and not wanting to give in, I reach down and slip my panties to the side myself, exposing my pussy to him. I hear his breath hitch and then he groans. "Say it, Norma." He's begging me to give in, and I feel like though I'm saying yes, he's the one who gave in first.

"Lick my pussy, Zach. Make me come . . . right here in the library where anyone could come upstairs and see you on your knees under the table. Is that what you want? That hint of danger?" Somehow, whispering the filthy words makes it easier to say them.

"Fuck, yes," he snarls, and then he dives into my pussy. He shoves my hands out of the way, pulling my panties to the side and spreading me wide open with his hands.

His tongue laps at me, tickling and teasing along my lips and then around my clit. I gasp at the onslaught, the sensations so good, but mixed with the risk of getting caught, it's so much more. I never knew that would be such a turn-on, but it is.

He moves his attention to my clit and sucks hard. I have to cover my mouth to stifle the moan bubbling up in my throat, threatening to loudly let loose. Zach chuckles against me, the vibrations adding a new feeling to his ministrations. "That's it, Brat. Let yourself go. You know you're loving every second of this just as much as I am. I want to see that soft Norma coming undone for me."

I grab at his hair, trying to get him back where I want him without answering the challenge of just how much I'm loving this. Because I am, I so am.

He licks a long line from my entrance to my clit and then sucks my clit into his mouth, using his tongue to flick against it fast and hard in the vacuum he's created around my tender bud. The world pulls tight for a moment, centered on my core, and then it explodes in a flash of white light.

My hips shake and my thighs quiver as I come for the first time from a man's touch. From Zach's touch. My body clenches and then sags as the orgasm washes over me in waves. I think I'm quiet, though right now, I don't really care.

Zach lays one last kiss to my clit, and I shudder, pulling away. "Too sensitive. Fuck."

He moves my panties back in place and lays a gentle pat to my mound, eyes looking up at me from under the table. "Never met a girl as sassy as you are, Brat.

Never had one as tasty either. You're like fucking honey."

His eyes are glazed over, and I wonder if I look as shell-shocked as he does. I don't know what just happened or what it means. Maybe it doesn't mean anything, but it was amazing.

He climbs out from under the table and bends down to kiss me. I can taste myself on his lips. He smirks. "See? You're fucking delicious."

He stands up, and I can see him, thick and hard inside his jeans. I reach out to touch him, cupping his length through the denim, wanting to pleasure him the way he just did me.

He seems to read my desire on my face because he takes my hand, pulling me to my feet and guiding me over to the endcap of one of the rows of books.

Zach licks my ear, making me whimper. "I thought so. You dressed up so sweet and innocent, giving me attitude . . . but you've got a dirty side, don't you?"

I tremble, my hips grinding on their own against his cock, and I bite my lip before admitting, "Maybe."

"Get on your knees, Norma." His tone is hard, something different from before but still with that undercurrent of a light dare.

I obey but can't help but sass him. "No jokes about me sucking you off or making me beg for the privilege?"

He cups my jaw in his rough palm. "Fuck that. If you want to suck my cock, I'm not gonna risk your ire and screw up this chance. I'll shut my fucking trap, bite back any words I might have, and thank God for the opportunity to be in your hot, sassy mouth."

I can't help but smile at the odd twist of compliment he just bestowed on me. Most people, guys especially, don't even consider shutting down their mouthiness. No, they just want me to stop mine. But Zach's different. He seems to like my mouth. Well, if that's the case, I'm going to make him fucking love it.

I undo his jeans, letting them fall wide open and pulling his boxer briefs down to let his cock free. He's . . . huge and gorgeous. I should've known. Football god like him would have an amazing cock to go along with it. Some people get all the blessings. Right now, I'm sure fucking glad though.

His thickness is a bit intimidating, so I lick around the head, teasing him and tasting him. I let my tongue slide along the length of his shaft, from root to tip, and then I take the plunge, filling my mouth with as much as I can take. My lips stretch wide, and I have to pull back, letting my saliva coat him inch by inch as I take him deeper, exploring the limits of my mouth and then my throat.

I find a rhythm, three shallow thrusts and then a slow, deep one that makes him groan in pleasure. The fourth time I do that, his hands tangle into my hair and my silk scarf headwrap falls off.

Zach grins mischievously. "Wait. Wait." I pop off his cock, surprised to hear him say that. But then he bends down and grabs the silk scarf.

"What are you gonna do with that?" I ask, not sure I like where this is headed.

But his smile is soft. "Give me your hands." I obey slowly, and he grabs my wrists in his massive hand before slipping the scarf around one wrist and then the other, loosely looping them together behind my back. It's not tight, and I could get out if I wanted to, but I find that the thought of being restrained is rather erotic. Like the thought of getting caught. I don't think I would want to be full-on, tied down at his mercy, just like I don't actually want someone to catch us and watch. But the fantasy of it, so close but not quite real, is somehow extremely sexy.

"You good?" Zach asks, a light in his eyes.

In answer, I suck him back into my mouth, moaning against his heated flesh. Looking up through my lashes, I can see that he's gripping the bookcase behind me so hard his knuckles are going white. He's trying to let me lead here, let me take him. But suddenly, the thought of his being in charge is rather enticing. Another thing I thought I wouldn't be into. I feel like I'm learning more about myself tonight than ever before.

I lick a lazy circle around his head, knowing he's on the edge and liking that I'm doing that to him. "Zach?" I whisper.

He grunts. "Yeah, Brat?" and his cock jumps, bumping against my upper lip.

"Fuck my mouth," I tell him, a little louder so that I'm sure he hears me. I'm ballsy as fuck, but I don't know if I can say that twice.

His smirk is full of delight, and he feeds me his cock in one smooth stroke, deep into my mouth. His hands don't leave the bookcase. Instead, he uses the leverage to loom over me, forcing me to look up, which lets him into my throat even easier.

"Fuck, Norma. Swallow my cock, take me deep," he says, getting a bit loud. I whimper against his skin, the sound a warning to be quiet.

He grimaces, forcing back his moans, and picks up the pace. His cock pumps into my mouth, sloppy with the combination of my saliva and his pre-cum, and I try to swallow it all down in preparation for what I know is coming. I can feel a drop running down my chin, but with my hands tied, I can't wipe it away. The trickle ends and I realize it's dripped onto my shirt.

But Zach doesn't stop, closer and closer with every stroke. And then he slips further into my throat and I feel the pulses as he comes, his hot cum filling my mouth as I fight to gulp it down. He cups the back of my head with one hand, holding me deep as his cock jerks over and over.

He throws his head back in release, his mouth open in a silent roar before a shudder runs through his whole body. It's a powerful sight to see him unfettered, and I wonder if this is why he was looking at me so glazed earlier. I wonder if he got this kind of joy from watching me come. The thought makes me smile.

Slowly, his head falls forward and his eyes meet mine. "Fuck, Brat. That was . . . fuck."

I like that he's speechless, that maybe I'm not some

orally super-skilled football groupie, but I did that to him, and judging by the look in his eyes, he fucking loved it.

I smirk at him. "Might have to expand your vocabulary a bit for the next paper," I tease.

He laughs. "You fucking brat. I think you sucked all of my vocabulary words out of my cock. Get up here." He pulls back, slipping his softening cock into his jeans before pulling me to stand in front of him.

I'm expecting him to untie me, but he kisses me first, apparently having no qualms about tasting himself on my tongue. I don't have any squeamishness about it either, and I actually rather like the dirty thought that he tastes like me, I taste like him, and our flavors are co-mingled within our kiss. But after a moment, he pulls back and spins me in place.

He makes quick work of the loopy knot in the silk scarf and then spins me back around.

"We should go. I don't know about you, but I have an eight AM class tomorrow," he says, though his tone says he wants to stay right here. Just that little hint resolves the whisper of doubt, of question in my mind and heart.

I smile. "Get some sleep. Eight tomorrow night again?" I hold my breath for a split second until he agrees.

"Definitely. See you tomorrow, Norma." His grin is wide as he struts out of the library.

It's not until he's gone and I'm alone that I think, *What the fuck did I just do?*

CHAPTER 7

ZACH

*S*he freaked out. I knew she would. But in the four days since that first bit of oral exchange, of the sexual variety, not our usual banter, I've managed to calm Norma down. I knew she'd have second thoughts, could tell she was inexperienced, but fuck if that didn't make me love it even more, that such a sassy spitfire could be so innocent but somehow push just the right buttons and let me push her too. Buttons I didn't even know I had.

I've had sex, though not nearly to the manwhore scale Norma thinks. But none of it compared to what Norma and I did in that library.

In public. Where anyone could've come up to see.

With her hands tied, at my mercy as I fucked her mouth.

No, that was on a whole different level.

So the next night, when she'd come in, ready to argue that we go back to a more professional level of tutor-

tutoree, I'd been expecting it. Her doubts, her fears, all masked in vinegar and snark.

The battle had been fierce and many bites had been given, but in the end, I'd won. Mostly.

"Are you sure about this?" Norma asks, looking at me like I've lost my ever-loving mind. "I mean, no one knows shit and we could just keep on meeting in the library. No need to throw a parade or anything."

We're standing outside the school food court, where we're about to go in and grab a slice of pizza for lunch.

This shouldn't be a big deal.

But it's such a big fucking deal. And we both know it.

It's part of my reassurance to her that I'm not just looking for some convenient pussy for the semester, some acknowledgement of the fact that I can't date anyone else when I'm supposedly dating Norma, cover story and all. I hate that it took me damn near flunking English to meet her, hate that there's this question lingering over our heads. But I wouldn't change a thing.

The fact is, I *am* dating Norma. And she's probably the least convenient pussy around me at any given time. Which might be why I want it so damn much.

"You don't get a choice here, unless it's cheese or sausage, because we're getting lunch," I say, making sure that she hears the lack of options here. She needs this, both the public acknowledgement and for me to force the issue and push her buttons a little because I know that even when we study and spend every night at the library touching and exploring, my fingers deep inside her or her lips wrapped around me again, she's questioning whether it's real. All because the setup was fake.

She grins, and I can see the devil in her eyes. "What if I say sausage and we head on over to my place so I can get my taste?" She glances down at my cock, knowing it doesn't take much to get me rock-fucking-hard for her.

I adjust myself, squeezing a bit hard to let the pinch of pain deflate my cock. "God damn it, Brat. Lunch. Let's go."

I open the door for her, and she steps inside, back held straight and shoulders squared. She looks like the tiniest warrior fairy ever, ready for battle. She stops just inside the door, and I stop beside her to take her hand. I look down at our clasped hands, and she looks up at me. She baits me. "Welcome to the funeral of your social standing, Football God."

The fire in her eyes belies the fact that she's nervous. She's not worried about my social standing. She's worried that this is going to lead to some 'who's that girl' situation and that she'll be on the losing end of the spectrum against the cheerleader types. Maybe for some guys, that'd be the case, but not me. Definitely not now.

Now, my type is a sassy, snarky little redhead who makes me work for every damn inch of her submission and then falls apart in a gorgeous shattering of sparks when I earn it. It's fucking addicting and I want it all the damn time.

I lead her across the cavernous room. If this were a Hollywood movie, a hush would fall over the crowd of people, chairs would screech as people turned to stare, and jaws would drop. None of that happens because it's just a college food court, and for the most part, people are buried in their own work and food.

We grab our pizzas and cokes, and she does get sausage, though I think it's mostly so she can take big, mean-looking chomps of it as a pseudo-threat to my manhood. Which she does as soon as we sit down at a table for two.

"You that hungry for sausage, Brat?" I tease, letting her know that she's not fooling me and that I'm on to her transparent symbolism.

"Ravenous. Wish I could eat the whole damn thing in one gulp right now," she says with a wink. Then she grabs her drink, letting her tongue slip out to catch the straw and then taking a cheek-hollowing suck.

It's an almost comical caricature of flirting, but damned if it doesn't set me off anyway because I know she's doing it intentionally to irritate me. "Keep it up and you'll get to," I promise her.

She tosses her napkin to her plate, grabbing the edges of her tray like she's ready to bolt out of here, but I lay a staying hand on hers. "After lunch."

She sighs and sits back in her chair. "Okay, bullshit aside, Zach. Why are we doing this? There's no need, really. The whole" —she lowers her voice to barely a whisper— "cover story was a just-in-case scenario." She looks around the room. "You know, if someone saw us and questioned why we're hanging out. But we don't have to invite people to the fucking wedding by showing up in the middle of the day to the most populous place on campus."

As if to prove her words, a guy bumps along the edge of the table as he passes by.

I weave my fingers through hers, holding her hand on the tabletop. "I know. And as much as I appreciate your help and your agreeing to that stupid fucking idea, I don't want to be the asshole who keeps you like some dirty little secret. You're better than that. And I figured you'd be the first person to stand up and demand to be treated like a damn queen. So why the hesitation? Unless you don't want to be public with me?"

Admittedly, the thought hurts and is something I hadn't considered. I mean, technically, dating a 'football god' is a good thing for most girls, but I'm well aware that Norma isn't most girls and can likely see problems coming a mile away that no one else would. Hell, she could probably drum some up if need be with her sharp mouth.

She bites and then purses her lips, cheekily challenging me. "What if I like being your dirty little secret?"

I growl, leaning forward, my voice thick. "Do you want to date me for real, Norma?"

She must hear the serious tone in my voice because all humor leaves her eyes as she nods. "Yes. I'm just scared."

I nod back. "I get that, but I'm here. I want to date you, for real. We're doing this together." She seems reassured. Serious talk done, I let the light back into my eyes. "Now, about that 'dirty little secret.' You won't *be* one, but we can sure as fuck *have* some dirty little secrets. That work?"

She leans forward. "Actually, there's something I've been meaning to tell you, but I wasn't sure how to."

My cock thickens in my pants at her words, and my brain starts shooting off in every imaginable direction, thinking she's about to tell me some dirty fantasy she wants to enact. Whatever it is, I'm on fucking board. "Tell me anything."

She tries to pull her hand away, but I clench it tighter, wanting the connection when she says whatever this is, holding her in place, close to me, though the table separates us.

"Zach, what we've been doing in the library . . . has been great. Better than great. But—"

Oh, shit. There's a 'but.' I hadn't considered this sentence was gonna have a 'but' in it.

"But I feel like I should tell you . . . I'm a virgin." She lets out a whoosh of air with the whispered word, and it takes my brain a minute to process what she just said.

"A virgin?" I parrot back quietly, disbelieving. She looks down at the pizza, like she can't meet my eyes. I use my free hand to tilt her chin up, locking her in place with my gaze. "All this sass, all this sexiness, all this mouthy brattiness . . . and you've never had a man inside you?" I ask, running my thumb along her full bottom lip. Her tongue peeks out to wet her lips and she catches the tip of my thumb too.

"Do you want me to be your first?" I ask, though my tone is more begging for the privilege.

"Fuck, yes," Norma moans, the words breathy.

"Let's go . . ." I say, standing up and taking her hand. Normally, I'd be the nice guy who clears our table, throwing the trash away and returning the tray. But today, I've got places to be. Namely, inside my Brat. Right the fuck now.

I drag her outside and around the corner of the building, a small concession to not fucking her up against the glass of the building's front. Instead, I press her up against the brick, caging her in my arms and taking her mouth in a kiss.

Her hands grab my T-shirt, her nails digging slightly into my chest for a split second before she fists the fabric, holding me in place. "Fuck, Norma. I'm gonna fuck you right here in the quad if we don't get out of here."

She sputters as I press off the building, pulling her by the hand. "We can go to my apartment. It's just off campus. We can even walk there."

I shake my head. "Oh no, Norma. I'm fucking you at *our* place . . . the library."

She argues the whole way there, and I let her rage and rile, knowing that once I get her there, she'll want it just like that.

I go not to our usual corner but to a quiet study zone room on the third floor instead. She huffs as I press her to the closed door, her head turned so she can see me even with her cheek against the wood.

I'm running on instinct here, letting what I honestly feel is the right choice pour from my lips to her ear. "I'm fucking you here, Brat. In our place. Not some cheap hotel room or a frat party bedroom, and not your sweet, innocent bedroom at home. Not this time. You deserve your first time to be great, and I can give that to you, right here where we met, where we belong."

"Someone's gonna see us," she pleads, even as she arches her back, rubbing her ass along the length of my cock. Her body is telling me exactly what she wants. It's like she's in a war between what she knows is the 'right' thing to do and what she really wants. What she wants every time we do something naughty here.

I grind against her, growling in her ear. "Listen to me. Just be quiet or cover your mouth if you have to, and no one will have a reason to come check the room."

"Fuck . . . that feels good," she whimpers as my hand cups her pussy.

"I can make your first time so good, Norma. Fill you up and rub your little clit until you come all around me." I spin her around, yanking her shirt and bra off and pressing her bare back against the door. "So fucking pretty, Brat." I dip down, taking her nipple into my mouth as I cup her tit, holding it up to my mouth.

The need is burning me up from the inside. We've been building up to this, day by day, conversation by conversation, touch by touch. And I can't wait anymore.

I pull her over to the big library table, yanking her shorts and panties down in one swoop as she kicks her shoes off. "Up you go . . ." I tell her as I help her lie down. I pull my T-shirt over my head and reach for the button of my jeans. Norma makes a mewling sexy kitten sound and I look up.

She's watching me, just as hungry as I am. I realize with a start that this is the first time I've seen her fully nude. I've pulled her shirt up and sucked her tits, I've spread her wide on a chair and eaten her out, and I've fingered her against more bookshelves than I can count.

But this is different. This is Norma, my Brat, spread wide and naked, every vulnerability exposed without armor, ready to take me for the first time. I take a mental snapshot of her writhing on the tabletop for me. It's a fucking honor and I can't wait. But she doesn't want my sweet words right now. That's not who she is, not who we are, at least not right now.

"You ready? You want to get fucked for the first time in the library, Norma? Behind a door that doesn't lock. Anyone could just waltz right in here." She bites her lip and tilts her head back, looking at the door upside down. I grab her ankles and pull her to the edge of the table, not sure it'll hold us both. Her legs spread wide around my hips, and I finish unbuttoning my jeans, shoving them down, and then my boxer briefs follow.

I take my cock in hand, pumping the shaft a few times as she watches. "Say it," I order her.

She grins, and I already can't wait to hear what she's gonna say. "Yes, Zach. I want you to fuck me, right here where anyone could walk by that tiny window in the door and see you balls-deep in my virgin pussy. You think you can handle that?" All sass and brattiness and challenge. I fucking love it.

I groan as pre-cum leaks from my tip at her words, and I use it to smooth my hand's way up and down my rock-hard length. I tease my head along her clit, not entering her yet but wanting to feel some part of her pussy against my cock. "Just think . . . it's dangerous, but it's a rush, isn't it?" She probably thinks I'm talking about the door. I'm really talking about her. She's fucking dangerous as hell, a sweet little innocent wrapped up in a prickly, ball-busting brat who drives me insane.

I aim lower, letting her feel me right against her entrance, and freeze. I lock eyes with her, wanting to watch to make sure she's okay with every bit of this. Her blue eyes shine back at me brightly, so I slide in ever so slowly. She's so tight. It's like nothing I've felt before, and I want to live buried in her pussy forever.

Just the head of my cock is in, but I pause, letting her get used to the feeling. Sex is like football. Sometimes, you need to no-huddle hurry up, but usually, it's better to take that extra heartbeat to make sure things are just right before you throw the ball downfield. "It's okay . . . do it. I'm so fucking ready, Zach," she encourages me. Touchdown.

I pull back and thrust further, breaking her cherry and causing her to cry out, the pain muffled by her forearm as she tries her best to stay quiet. I hold still, letting her adjust until the pain washes away and I start thrusting again slowly.

It's not only because she's a virgin that I'm taking my time. It's something else too. It's the look in her eyes as she starts to fuck me back a little, the challenge and the vulnerability all tied up in one as my cock turns the pain into the pleasure that rolls through her as she realizes she's taken a step that she can never retreat from. She gets more into it, thrusting with me, and her mouth drops open as my hips smack against hers and her pussy clenches around me.

"Oh, fuck, Zach," she whispers. "You feel so good inside me."

I look her in the eyes. "Norma, you feel good inside me too." She gasps as she realizes the depth of my words, her hands clasping as she holds them to her chest. It almost looks like she's praying, but the muffled sounds coming from her are more devilish than angelic.

I give her a hard stroke, holding deep inside her and grinding there for a second, then reach down to the floor to grab her panties. No scarf right now, though I know there's probably one in her bag, but I'm not leaving the glory of her pussy to get it. This will have to do. I take the silky scrap and wrap it around her wrists, feeding her hands through the leg holes. It's not a perfect restraint, but it never is. It's more the illusion of it that gets us both off.

Her fingers tangle and clasp again, the dark green of the panties bright against her fair and freckled skin, and she squeezes around me. It didn't mean anything when I tied up her wrists that first time. It was just something I felt, but now it's become one of our things, and it's so fucking sexy when she gives herself over to it and to me.

Her sweet tightness is doing me in, and somehow, she finds the strength to keep pushing into me, encouraging me to fuck her harder and give her more.

I slip my thumb to her clit, swirling it in tight circles, and she bucks beneath me. I lay a hand on the table next to her head, leaning over to get an up-close view of the first time she comes on my cock. This is something that will only happen the first time once, and I'm not going to miss a bit of it. She moans, louder than usual, but I'm sure not going to tell her to be quiet. Instead, I tell her, "Say it, Brat. Tell me what you want."

Her breath hitches, but her eyes are clear enough to meet mine. "Rub my clit, Zach. Fuck me hard until I come. I need to come before someone sees me."

"I see you, Norma." The words hang in the air a split second, and then she detonates all around me.

"Yes!" she rasps as her body convulses in waves. Her eyes roll back and her mouth opens in a silent scream. It's the prettiest thing I've ever seen.

My cock swells, and her tight pussy clenches around me one last time, pushing me over. "Fuck, Brat!" I fill her up, crashing with waves of white light as she milks me for every drop of cum before we both sag. I place a palm on either side of her head and bend down to sip at her lips softly. "You good?"

I feel her lips spread into a wide grin. "No, I'm fucking fantastic." And then she giggles, that little girl sound I can pull from her every once in a while.

I agree with her. "Yeah, you are, Brat."

CHAPTER 8

NORMA

D ear Diary,

I'm pretty sure I've met my match. I wore that virgin badge so proudly, certain that any guy able to match my bites wouldn't stick around long enough to earn my cherry. Until Zach. Oh, yeah, I'd say I gave it to him, but it's more like he took it from me. Although I was damn sure willing . . . willing to do it in a public place, willing to let him loop my panties around my wrists, willing to let him say filthy things to me and say some of my own back, willing to let him fill me with his cock and cum. All that . . . so fucking willing.

He seems pretty set on us actually dating too, not just the secret cover story. I'll admit that I don't fully trust that. His words seem heartfelt, but I just can't believe that a guy like him wants someone like me.

But I'm playing along either way, dating or 'dating', and really tutoring him. He got the B he needed on his Idolatry in Paradise Lost *paper, a B-plus, in fact. I think it was worthy of an A, but the professor probably wasn't expecting A-quality work from him. Harsh but true.*

He's even been texting me pictures of him, full of sweaty workout hair and goofy grins with captions like 'You wanna kiss now?' I didn't tell him that I'd happily kiss him when he's all gross. I sent him back a picture of me holding my crinkled nose with a caption of 'No thanks, stinky boy.' But the teasing banter continues between us, sometimes juvenile, sometimes sexy, and sometimes sharp. I love every bit of it.

I've met my match.

———

THE LAST NOTES OF SUNSET ARE JUST DISAPPEARING INTO the horizon as I unlock my apartment door and head inside. Yeah, it's Sunday, and yes, most people have a history of taking Sundays off.

Zach and I, though . . . well, it's only been two Sundays, ten days since he took my virginity, but Sunday is already my favorite day of the week. Ten days . . . and he's fucked me nearly every day possible.

The only days we've missed were this past Friday and Saturday, since he had an away game. But I watched the game, only the third football game I've ever watched that wasn't a newspaper assignment, tuned in the whole time as Zach ripped apart the other team for five touchdowns. Sure, the other guys on the team helped, but I can tell he's the glue that holds them together. A responsibility he's told me he takes very seriously.

Today, after getting his text, we met up again . . . this

time at the stadium, shortly after the team left from their post-game wrap-up. We reviewed class notes and how to structure an argumentative essay in the home team locker room before Zach pushed me up against the lockers and finger-fucked me while pinching and kneading my nipples.

We've yet to have sex in a 'regular' place. Besides the stadium, we've tried out many of the musty old parts of the library, and once in a closet while people walked by, oblivious to him thrusting his cock into me with his hand covering my mouth.

I keep thinking we're going to get busted, that we should either stop this entirely or at least be a little more discreet. Maybe use my empty bedroom instead of hiding in the shadows of the library.

But every time he touches me, every moment we're together, I'm unable to think about anything else. I'm willing to take any risk to be with him. Hell, the risk of being with him in those wild places is half the fun. Okay, maybe not half. It's mostly fun because of Zach, but the chance of getting caught definitely adds to it.

He seems to be telling the truth about wanting us to really be a thing, though that's still so hard for me to believe. I mean, the nerd and the jock? How fucking cliché is that? People would be more likely to believe it was some tutoring cover story than that we actually like each other and have things in common to talk about.

But the way his eyes light up when he sees me, the way he shares with me and the little things he does—like actually fucking study—tell me that this is real, that he sees me as more than just a fun fuck.

The thought warms my heart, and then I hear the ding of a reminder on my phone. Sunday evening . . . phone call time. I dig my phone out of my bag, plopping on the couch to call my big brother, Liam.

It rings a few times, then I hear the call connect before Liam's voice rings out. "Norma Jean Blackstone, is that you? I thought something had happened to you since you haven't called to bust my balls in so damn long."

I grin. "Oh, my apologies, brother. You need me to insult you a bit? I'd be happy to oblige," I tease, intending to start listing his faults in a humorous manner, but the words don't come. And then I realize how soft of a lob he's throwing me, and I laugh as I tell him, "Besides, isn't it Arianna's job to bust your balls now?"

Liam laughs a hearty chuckle. "That it is, little sis. And she does a fine job of keeping me in line, no worries there."

"How is she? I haven't seen her around, though I usually don't since we don't have any classes together," I ask. Arianna is Liam's secretary-slash-girlfriend and she attends classes at the university with me. But that's where the similarities end. Arianna is stunning and made of steel, laser-sharp focused on business, and she somehow managed to actually fall in love with my arrogant brother.

"She's doing well, settled into her fall class schedule and set up her work schedule accordingly. I think she wants to have dinner soon, just the three of us. Unless there's a fourth you'd like to bring . . ." He lets the prying inquiry trail off.

"No . . . yes . . . well, kind of, I guess," I say with a laugh. "I'm not sure. I am seeing someone, but I don't know if we're at a dinner with the family stage yet."

I hear a crackle of leather and I can visualize Liam sitting down on the couch, probably shocked at my words. I'm not exactly a frequent dater so my admission is tantamount to telling him I'm nominated for a Pulitzer.

"My baby sister is growing up. I'm so proud of you, Norma Jean." His voice is pure sarcasm, much like mine usually is, but the sentiment is real, just like mine usually is too.

"Thanks, Liam. Your CEO-intern love story was rather inspirational and made me open to finding my true love. Just think how many relationships the Hallmark movie of your and Arianna's taboo affair will inspire." I'm totally full of shit about the movie, but they really did have a hard time at the office when their relationship came out. That seems to have settled down now, though, and I'm glad for them.

"Ha-ha, but if you tell Arianna that, she'd probably love it. She's a hopeless romantic. So, speaking of romance, what's the unlucky bastard's name?" His tone is casual, the insult smooth as silk, but I'm not a newbie to his games.

"Nice try, but I'm not telling you his name so you can run a background check on him. He's fine, I swear." I roll my eyes at his overprotectiveness, but I secretly love that Liam wants to protect me. I'd never let him know that though. "Besides, if he wasn't fine, I'd cut him off at the dick long before you'd get your chance."

Liam hisses through the phone. "Please, for the love of fuck, Norma . . . I do not want to hear you use the word *dick*. You're my baby sister and I remember when you were a cute little thing on the couch, watching cartoons. I can't handle you and . . . dicks."

It's a reasonable request, so I blatantly ignore it. "Why, Liam, if you don't like me saying 'dick', how about 'cock' or 'pussy' or—gasp—what about 'cunt'? He starts singing in my ear, *la la la la la la*, and I laugh. "Okay, okay, I'm done. Promise." I enjoy when we can have these little moments of childishness again because it reminds me of how close Liam and I have always been.

There was a rough patch for a while when Liam was finishing college and our dad made the mistake of telling Liam that he wasn't going to bring him up in the family business. Well, I'm not sure of the exact wording because I was still in elementary school, but basically, their relationship, which had already been tenuous, imploded. They rarely talk anymore, though I know Dad is proud of Liam's success. But even then, when Liam was refusing Dad's calls, he'd hang out with me, his whiny kid half-sister. He even chose to deal with my mom, his stepmother, to pick me up instead of coordinating it through Dad. Whatever their drama, we've always made it a priority to not let it affect our relationship, and that's something I'm thankful for.

Liam laughs once more and then sobers. "Seriously, though, does he treat you right? Make you happy?"

I smile, even though Liam can't see me. "Yes and yes. He's a good guy. I think you'd like him, but give me some time."

He sighs but agrees. "You got it, Sis. But if you really do have to chop his dick off, don't say a word and use your one phone call for me. I'll get you a lawyer."

I bark out a laugh, the thought absolutely preposterous, which makes Liam's entertaining it even funnier. I always press his buttons and give him shit, but it's a rare treat when he's on fire and shoots back just as much as I do. "Got it. Hey, I gotta go hit the books. Talk to you later?"

"Sure thing, Norma Jean. Bye." He hangs up and I disconnect on my end too.

It was fun to spar with Liam, but the thought of sitting around his table with Zach at my side for dinner is throwing me for a loop right now. There's a pit in my stomach that says don't ask for too much, but there's another part of me that says it sounds like a good outing.

That night, I dream about introducing Zach Knight, Football God, to my business-dry brother and dad. I wake up in the middle of the night with my heart racing, not sure if it's because the dream was going so well or so badly.

"SO, HOW'S THE TUTORING COMING?"

I look up from my story, a quick little no-brainer about an upcoming show the art department is doing, to see Erica sitting down next to me, keeping her voice low. "What do you mean?" I ask.

"I mean, can he tell the difference between a comma and an apostrophe?" Erica sarcastically hisses, rolling her eyes. "Milton, dammit! How's he doing on Milton?"

"Just fine. His grades have been better," I reply, inwardly cringing. Tutoring Zach on *Paradise Lost* has me reading it myself, of course, and the parallels between Milton's long-winded narrative on temptation and innocence lost and what I'm currently going through certainly haven't escaped me. "He doesn't like it, but I can't fault him there."

I grin for maximum effect, because I know almost nobody likes Milton. Still, it's a staple. Hopefully, Erica buys it, but as she keeps studying me, I grow frightened. Here's where she's going to bust me, I just know it.

Still, I'm not lying. Zach's grades have improved on the two papers he's recently written. And no, I didn't do the work for him. He's more than capable, with plenty of brains to go with his sublime body. He's just been trying to bullshit his way through a class without even taking the time to read the Cliff Notes.

Erica purses her lips, then nods. "Okay. Listen, keep up the good work. I know Zach's hard, but you seem to be on top of him."

More like underneath, in front of, and on my knees with . . . but

I've been on top too, I think, trying not to choke on my own horrified laughter. Did I almost say that?

"Are you using the cover story or has no one caught on? I mean, surely, someone has noticed the two of you in the library every night, right?" Erica asks.

Before I can stop the words, they shoot out. "God, I hope not." I think back to our study sessions and how careful we always are. We've never spotted anyone near us at all, but that doesn't stop us from enjoying the 'might get caught' taboo factor.

Erica is taken aback by my answer for a split second and then her eyes narrow as she analyzes me. I'm reminded of why she's the boss of the school paper. She's shrewd, with great instincts, and great at reading people. A flush steals up from my chest to my face, but I keep my mouth shut.

"You're fucking him, aren't you?" Erica asks, clucking her tongue. "Damn, I thought you'd be immune, but I guess no one really is."

I still don't deny or confirm her suspicions.

"Look, just be careful here, Norma. I really didn't mean for you to get tangled up with Zach like that. Figured the cover story was a last-ditch effort if someone caught up to you. Honestly, I figured you were a bit stronger than his flirtations too."

I shrug. "He's nice, and we've been spending a lot of time together." Even though I still haven't said yes, that we're seeing each other, she gets the drift.

"Do what you want, girl. But that guy is a manwhore,

and I can't imagine that you're into that. Don't let him play you with slick words and sweet nothings. You need to come out the other side of this unscathed."

Nodding, I tell her, "I hear you. I swear, I'm good. Promise."

She purses her lips like she doesn't believe me, but she holds her tongue. But her words continue to ring in my mind just like she intended.

Erica leaves, and I quickly finish my article before rushing to the library. I'm early and do my own studying until Zach shows up. I'm immersed in my math assignment when I feel arms wrap around me from behind. My instinct is to elbow back, maybe bite at the hands trying to cover my mouth, but then I realize it's Zach and settle, a giggle escaping my mouth.

"What are you doing? This is a library, you know!" I chastise him, though he knows I love it.

He grins, taking my hand and leading me up to the fourth floor where we drop our bags on our usual table.

Over the next few hours, we study, we flirt, and I come all over Zach's fingers, bucking for every stroke. But Liam's and Erica's words echo in my ear like opposing drums. *One . . . be happy. Two . . . he's playing you.*

And as we go over the argument between angel and fallen angel in book six, I wonder if I, too, will end up discarded when my usefulness is over.

CHAPTER 9

ZACH

"Come on, put some leg into it!" Coach Buckley says as I scramble through the cones, stopping and heaving a long bomb downfield. It's a missile, sixty-five yards, that flies in a beautiful arc to drop into Lenny's arms.

"That's how you do it! Be ready to do it again, just like that, for this weekend's game." Coach yells, excited. "Jake, you're up!"

I watch as Jake takes the snap, dropping back, dodging the orange cone, and chucking it downfield to Lenny.

"Fuckin' A!" Jake says, pumping his fist as his ball hits Lenny in stride. "That's a starter's arm there!"

I say nothing as Jake continues his celebration. I really don't care about his bragging as long as Coach isn't considering that Jake might be right. But Coach Jefferson isn't even watching Jake's passes. Sixty-five yards on a two-step stop is great, but there's more to the game than being able to throw it downfield. Practice continues, and afterward, Jake's still riding high as we get changed in the locker room.

"So, Knight, you feeling the heat about losing your spot yet?" Jake asks as I come out of the shower. He's got a big shit-eating grin on his face like his takeover is imminent. "Because it won't be long before you feel me coming up on your ass."

A few of the guys instantly stop to see if this gets out of hand, knowing there's already animosity between us. "Snake, I'm naked and fresh out of the shower. Do you really want to talk about coming up on my ass? I already told you, if you want the starting job, show what you can do. Until then, keep holding that clipboard on the sidelines."

Maybe that last part was a bit too harsh, but I don't need him in my face, talking shit. It'd be different if he were just fucking around. But when he says it, it's out of sheer jealousy and animosity. He really does think he's the better player, the better leader for our team, and that he deserves the QB gig just because he's played longer, as if it's something you earn with seniority, not skill.

And while I may be a cocky asshole, I earned my spot as the QB with hard work, something my dad instilled in me from day one. I still remember his telling a Peewee football-sized me that 'hard work beats talent when talent doesn't work hard.' It'd been a few years later, after putting forth the effort to really learn the game that I loved, that we realized I might have some real talent. But he never let me rest on my laurels, insisting that I had a responsibility to keep working hard to make the best of the gift given to me.

And I've worked my ass off, on and off the field, running myself to the ground to be physically better than I was yesterday and striving to gain the coaches' and players' respect. Something tantrum-throwing Jake will never have.

Jake's face turns a deep brick red as he stomps out of the locker room. I look around and realize damn near the whole team was watching the exchange. "Show's over, guys. Same damn rule stands today as it did yesterday and the day before that. We're all here to do our fucking best and earn our way. There are no handouts and we could all lose our spots if we fuck off."

There are murmurs of agreement, and Lenny gives me high-five, bro-ing out with a "Fucking A, man. That's the truth." Everyone is still pulling their shit together, the long practice wearing everyone down. But I'm ready to get out of here and get to Norma. I quickly toss on sweats and a T-shirt and run my fingers through my hair. It's nothing fancy, but we've gotten more comfortable around each other and practicality dictates that my baggy grey sweats are way easier for her to slip her hand inside for a bit of hand action. In contrast, she's taken to wearing little cotton skirts that twirl out when she spins, and more importantly, they flip up easily for me to get at her pussy.

I'm distracted by my dirty thoughts as I walk across the parking lot, taking a direct path toward the library instead of following the winding sidewalk path. But I'm broken out of my mindlessness by a revving engine.

At the last minute, I look to my right and see Jake gunning for me in some twisted version of chicken. I don't think he's actually going to hit me, but he seems intent on scaring the shit out of me. I jump out of the way, and as he flies by, I can see the evil grin on his face so I yell out at him. I doubt he heard me, though, because he doesn't even slow as he peels out of the lot. In his fucking Mercedes. The one I'm sure his dad bought for him. I don't begrudge him nice things, but it's just another symbol of his being handed everything on a silver platter and not knowing how to handle it when he doesn't get what he wants.

I'm tempted to chase after him, yank him out of that fancy-ass car, and set him straight on the proper way to behave with teammates. Knowing that's probably the worst thing I could do right now in the mood I'm in, I hoof it straight to the library, hoping that seeing Norma will be the distraction I need.

But even as the fall evening air blows against my over-heated skin, I can't let the anger go. Seeing the way Jake looked at me as he gunned his engine has me more and more pissed with every step. I'm going to have to deal with him eventually, not just let Coach handle it. I'm going to have to challenge him face to face the way he keeps doing me. I'm definitely fucking willing to do that, but I have to be smart about it. A QB who flies off the handle on a teammate isn't attractive to coaches or scouts, whether it's him or me.

When I get to the library, Norma is waiting for me in the lobby of the library. She looks cute and sexy, wearing a frayed-hem denim skirt and a white blouse. Her hair is pulled back at the nape of her neck and she has a folded red scarf wrapped around her head. And if I were more focused right now, my cock would already be at full staff from seeing her lips, which are satiny-smooth with bright red lipstick, an obvious sign that she plans on blowing me tonight. She turns to show off her shoes, a pair of polka-dot heels that might bring her up to five-seven when she stands tall, and I know she wore them just for me. She's got a whole naughty modern 50s pinup vibe going on. To top it off, I know that underneath her skirt are some sexy silk panties. She's worn them almost every *study* session we've had since she discovered how much I like them on her.

She's saying so much with her clothes, and I get the message loud and clear and appreciate the effort she put into dressing up for me. If only I were in the mood . . . but after the locker room shit and then nearly getting run over by an asshole who's trying to take my job, sex is actually, for once, the last thing on my mind.

We head upstairs to our spot on the fourth floor. "Whoa," she says as I try and fail to avoid slamming my books onto the table. I drop into my seat, and the wood actually creaks dangerously under the strain. "You okay?"

"Yeah, just . . . a fucking asshole tried to run me over in the parking lot," I growl, reaching for my dog-eared copy of Milton. "Don't sweat it. It's fine. I'll get it figured out."

Norma looks at me for a minute, then shakes her head. I'm not sure if she realizes I'm being literal about the near-miss with the car. She reaches over and puts her hand on mine. I've got big hands, the better to grip a football with, and hers looks almost like a kitten's paw on top of mine. "I'm sure you can figure it out, but talk to me. What happened?"

I look into her eyes, and before I can let any self-doubt stop me, I nod. "I'd rather not do it here. Maybe we could go for a walk?"

Her lips lift in a small smile. "I've got one better. C'mon." She grabs her stuff and I follow suit. Holding hands, I let her lead me out of the library and out to the parking lot.

She digs keys out of her bag and unlocks a new black Volkswagen Jetta that sparkles in the parking lot lights. I whistle. "Wow."

"Gift from my dad," she says, and I remember that her family is rich enough that my potential pro-ball money might not even qualify as pocket change to them. I'm struck by the fact that, in contrast to whiny, entitled Jake, Norma doesn't seem effected by her family's wealth. Sure, she's had opportunities afforded by their funds, but she's got good core values and is a good person under-neath the privilege.

I get in as she starts up the engine and we pull out. I don't ask where we're going. I don't really care. I just want to get away. But as she drives, I get the sense she's taking us away from campus. "So, talk to me," she says as we get on the highway. "What's got you worked up today?"

"Jake Robertson," I reply, sighing as I lean back. "Sorry. I shouldn't have been so pissed off about it all."

"No, it's okay," Norma reassures me. "Who is he?"

"My backup on the team," I admit, looking out the window as the lights go by, lulling me into a trance. It's nice in her car, quiet except for the motor, and the soft scent of her perfume somehow calms me. "He's got issues with me."

"Why's that?" Norma asks. When I shift around, she glances over, her voice serious. "Zach, this isn't for the paper. This is just for you."

I nod, even though that wasn't even on my mind. "Jake's a redshirt senior. You know what that means?"

"I've heard the term, so kind of. He's actually been at school five years? Why'd he redshirt a year?"

"When he got here, the team had two guys ahead of him, good players. One went pro in Canada, and the other got some chatter from the League but ended up coaching high school ball instead. He's at some uber-competitive 6A school in Texas. So Jake redshirted that first year to study, fill out, and get a solid year of college under him. He backed up the younger of the two guys for a year and actually started his sophomore year."

"How'd he do?" Norma asks, and I shake my head, snorting derisively.

"Let's just say when I showed up for freshman ball the next year, it was a serious fight between me and him for the starting job. That burned him hard, especially since I was just a freshman who, in his eyes, hadn't paid his dues. But then when the team went out and lost the first five games, Coach Jefferson took a chance and put me in. I lit it up, and I've had the job since."

"So, what made the difference?" Norma asks. "I mean, I'm pretty ignorant of football besides that you're one hell of a player." She smiles with the compliment, and I give her a half-hearted lift of my lips to show I appreciate it.

I shrug. "He's not bad, and it wasn't all on him. The team just didn't have all the right pieces then, and it's a team for a reason. But there's got to be a leader on the field, and he gets rattled and off his game easily," I tell her. "Then he starts making mistakes and can't take the heat when it falls on his shoulders. He blames everyone else when it's a shared final score, win or lose. He just made everyone play worse overall. Anyway, this is his last shot, so he's getting frustrated and desperate. I'm not worried about his taking my spot—that's not fucking happening—but if he keeps pushing my buttons, he's gonna get decked. Shit, that might even be part of his plan, but I'm trying to keep my cool."

I huff, shaking my head. "I can't believe he actually tried to buzz me with his fucking car." Norma gasps, and I think she realizes I wasn't exaggerating. She looks me up and down, like she's checking me for injuries, and I reassure her. "I'm fine. Really. Just pissed me off because that was fucking dangerous, and he was grinning like it was some big joke."

"Shit," she breathes. "Why does it matter to him that much? Does he actually think he has a shot at the pros?"

"No, it's too late for that for him. Besides, Jake's family is pretty well off, and from what I've heard in the locker room, he's going to be working at his father's company. I think he just wants to have that thing to hang his hat on that *he* did, something that's his own and not his father's."

"Is that why you play? To have something of your own? What's your family think about all this?" she asks.

I smile a big smile at that, years of my parents' cheering in the stands coming back in an instant. "They love football too. Probably why they put me in it when I was barely bigger than a football. They've been supportive all along, but this year, especially, with all the interest from the pro scouts, they've been telling me to get my degree first and play pro later." I mimic my dad's voice because I can totally hear him saying that, so vivid it's like he's here, but it's only because he's said it dozens of times. "I'm the first in my family to go to college. I used the golden ticket football afforded me, and I plan to use it to get to the next phase too."

"Then what? What's the plan after the pros?" She asks it naturally, but it takes me by surprise. No one ever asks me that. Playing in the League is the goal, the final step, the be-all-end-all. You play until you're too injured or they won't offer you a contract, and then you fade off into obscurity. There is no plan for after, or at least not one that most folks give a shit about.

"Put my degree to work, I guess. I've got this year, plus one more, on my Sports Management degree. Figured that'd help me with my own contracts and negotiations in the pros, and then when I can't play, I can help other guys get fair deals. But it's all football, always football. It's all I've ever known, and I love it just the same today as I did when I was five. Maybe more."

"I'm just guessing here, but I think that's why you're better than Jake Robertson," she says.

I interrupt her, teasing and feeling better after getting everything off my chest and talking about my parents. "You don't even know if I'm better. You're just taking my word for it."

She laughs a bit. "Should I take it that you're full of shit then? That this Robertson guy is better than you?"

I growl. "No. I'm better than he is."

She nods. "Duh. Then as I was saying, I think you're better than him because you have such a passion for the game. It's not about making your own mark on the world to stand out of your dad's shadow. It's just about your love for football and leading the team to victory. You want what's best for all the guys, not just yourself."

I nod but then smirk. "Well, all the guys except for Robertson. He can drive that fancy fucking Mercedes off the road somewhere and never show up to practice again. I wouldn't be sad, wouldn't shed a tear. And we'd win games all the same without him." They're harsh words but tempered with the snobby humor in my voice. I don't actually wish harm to Jake. I just want him to get his shit in line.

She purses her lips, weighing my seriousness. "Oh, he's back, the cocky bastard who can do no wrong. Too much serious talk for you, caveman?" She makes a silly grunting noise to drive her point home, but it's too cute to be insulting.

I glance to the road, noting that there are no headlights

for miles, and lean across the console, breathing in her ear. "But you fucking love it when I go all 'caveman' on your bratty ass, don't you?"

She sticks her tongue out at me but admits, "Maybe."

"Stick that tongue out again, Brat, and I'm gonna put it to work," I warn her, but she doesn't back down. I knew she wouldn't. I hoped she wouldn't.

"Work?" She gulps, but I can see her eyes flick down to my groin.

"On dinner. Let's get something to eat. I'm starving," I say, delighted at the way she deflates that I didn't say something sexy. But I really do want to grab a bite. "And then after that, maybe you can stick that tongue out again for my cock, leave a nice ring of that pretty red lipstick on me like you're marking your fucking territory."

Norma signals, getting off the highway and pulling into a parking lot. "While door number two sounds delightful, I think I'll take door number one . . . a dinner date."

CHAPTER 10

NORMA

I know it's not a typical first date, where the well-dressed guy picks the nervous girl up and drives her to a restaurant for polite conversation. But this is us, and through some twist of fate, grabbing a bite to eat after a long drive is our actual first date. Not just meeting in the library or grabbing lunch in the food court. Not secret sexcapades or conversations about centuries-old poetry. Our first date is real conversation, connecting as Zach works out some sketchy shit with his team, and a steak dinner. Okay, and probably some racy action later, I think with a small smile.

But a secret thrill goes through my body when Zach holds the door open for me like a total gentleman and then takes my hand as we approach the hostess stand. He keeps the link until we reach the table and then he gestures for me to sit before sliding into the booth next to me. His muscular thigh is pressed against mine under the table, and when he places his palm along the bare stretch of skin below the hem of my skirt, I fully expect him to start working his way higher.

But he doesn't. He just rests it there, casually and comfortably, like it's the most natural thing in the world. And instead of sparks of arousal at his touch, I feel a warmth settle in my heart.

"What are you thinking?" Zach asks, his eyes scanning the menu.

I look over my own plastic-coated list of choices, glad that I'm not one of those girls that only eats organically paleo vegan or whatever. I think everything on this menu, including the menu itself, probably consists of beef. "I'm going for the Angus burger," I finally say. "Oh, and a strawberry milkshake."

He smiles, and I can't help but say the same thing I do every time I order a shake, though I keep it quiet so the next table over doesn't hear me. "*My milkshake brings all the boys to the yard . . .*" I can't sing for shit, but I add a little shoulder move to spice it up a bit.

Zach barks out a laugh, then leans in close, his growl in my ear. "You'd better not bring any boys to the yard, Brat. Just me. I'm the only one in your yard, and don't you forget it." He leans back, his eyes hard and hot as they glance over my face, now flushed from his words.

"What are you going to get?" I ask, disappointed that I don't have a snappy comeback, but when he looks at me like that, I swear my brain shuts down in favor of other body parts getting priority functioning.

He smirks, knowing he got me. "Sirloin and veggies,

with iced tea. Maybe a bit of your milkshake." I'm ninety-nine percent sure he's not talking about the frozen drink the waitress is going to bring.

Luckily, my brain is starting to be useful again and I fire back, "You think I'm gonna share my shake? Ooh, that's a big ask, Zach Knight. We'll have to see if you play your cards right to see if you can get a . . . *taste*."

Our shared smile is one of silly humor, but more importantly, it's one of finding someone to play with and have fun.

After ordering, we sit back and conversation flows easily. I don't want to get Zach riled up about Jake again, so I stick with checking in on his English progress. "So, how are your grades in English now? I know you've had several papers that were B or higher, but have you checked your overall? Your eligibility shouldn't be in jeopardy now, right?"

Zach grabs his phone from the table top and clicks for a second and then flashes the screen at me. He's logged into the university's app and the screen shows his current overall grade . . .75! "Oh, my gosh, Zach! That's great! Congratulations! By the time midterms roll around, you might even have a B if you keep up the hard work."

Zach looks at the screen like he can't believe it. "Not bad for a dumbass jock, huh?"

I smack his bicep. "Don't talk like that. You're not a dumbass and you know it. You said you did well in high school English and all your other college courses are going well. You're smart. You just checked out on *Paradise Lost* and that's totally understandable."

He smiles. "I know you're right. I've just always done better with a football in my hand than a book. I can get by, but I won't claim to be *smart*."

"I think you've got plenty of brains," I reply, slipping my hand around his bicep and holding him loosely, not forcing his hand to stay on my thigh but certainly not dissuading it either. "You're juggling college with football, and that's a lot. How big is your playbook?"

Zach thinks before answering. "Over a hundred plays easily, plus formation variations."

"And every week, you have to adjust that to the other team, right?" I continue. "Then you have to execute on the field, and you're making decisions in what, thirty seconds at a time?"

Zach nods. "Something like that, though we have an offensive coordinator who sends in plays."

"That takes brains, Zach. And before you tell me that there's a system, a formula to your plays and all, guess what? I've got a formula too when I write. My brother has a formula he uses when he looks at business deals. Sometimes, we even have to break the formula when our guts say to do so."

"Is that what you did with me? Break your formula?" He's teasing, but I can see the hint of realness to his question.

"I think we both broke our formulas here. But so far, I'm

thinking this play has gone pretty well." I raise one eyebrow, daring him to disagree.

His eyes trace down to my red lips, and he whispers, "Yeah, I'm pretty sure this audible is gonna lead to a touchdown."

I grin and whisper back, "Does football talk as seduction usually work for you?"

"Oh, yeah. Watch this . . ." He leans in close, his lips brushing my ear. Then he says, "Rally . . . six-nine . . . connect and smash."

A breathy sigh escapes my lips and then what he said filters through the fog of my arousal and I grin. "That's not even a thing, is it?"

He smirks like the cocky bastard he can be. "Not even close, but I'm not calling plays on the field. I'm calling plays on your body, and smashing into your sweet pussy sounds like the game-winning move."

I laugh at his arrogant outrageousness, our smiles mirrored on each other's faces. The waitress stops by, dropping off our food, and a pleasant tension fills each bite as we look forward to what's going to happen after dinner. It's another new change to our dynamic. Normally, when we meet up for studying, it seems the sex comes out of nowhere with no leadup. Oh, there's plenty of foreplay, but not like this.

I take a big bite of my burger and Zach grins. "I feel like we've been talking about football all night. Tell me . . . why journalism?"

He waits while I chew and swallow, using the moment to gather my thoughts. "I've always been inquisitive by nature, I guess. I like finding out about people, what makes them tick, what makes them do the things they do. And watching my dad, while he's a good guy, there's just so much behind-the-scenes shit that goes on. I think that in some cases, the public deserves to know what's happening with their friendly global corporate monopoly."

He nods. "You ever think about going into the family business? You said your brother started his own company too. But what about you?"

I shake my head. "Hell no. I like the nuances of business, but I like reporting on them, not directing the success or failure of the whole thing. My brother and dad are like two peas in a pod, though they'd kill me if they heard me say that. Both are super-driven and competitive, willing to work themselves to the bone, but with just enough charm that they're benign leaders of their companies, not cartoonish evil empire villains. Although it was touch-and-go there for a while with Liam, until he met Arianna. But she got him whipped into shape. I think you'd like him . . . now."

He looks at me in surprise. "Are you asking me to meet your family, Brat?"

The look of horror on his face has me stuttering. I didn't mean my comment like that, but he doesn't have to be so put off by the mere thought of meeting my brother. "No . . . no, I just meant, you two would get along, I think. But not like there's a family dinner I'm asking you to or anything . . ." I trail off, heat flushing my face and burning the backs of my eyes.

Zach realizes it and cups my cheek. "Shit. I'm sorry, Norma. I was just kidding . . . seriously. I would love to meet your infamous brother, and your mom and dad too, if you want. Let's have a whole fucking pony parade and I can meet them all if it'll make you not cry."

"No, it's fine. I'm sorry. You were just pushing my buttons like we always do. I'm not sure why that one just felt like a sting instead of a tease." I huff out a breath, letting my unexpected reaction go as I realize that it was only in my head. Just a momentary uprising of doubt. About myself or about Zach, I'm not sure which. Or maybe just about us. In the back of my mind, there's a whisper . . . *the jock and the nerd . . . so cliché*. But I force it away, knowing that Zach has done nothing to make me think he's not just as into this thing between us as I am.

CHAPTER 11

ZACH

*T*he drive is quiet as we head back to campus, and finally, I can't take it. "Pull over somewhere."

She looks at me questioningly but does as I say, finding a dark side road that's deserted and stopping the car. "Now what?" she asks, and I can hear the hesitation in her voice.

I get out and walk around the driver's side of the car, opening her door and leading her out. I lift her up and set her on the hood of the car. Her skirt rides up as I step between her knees, forcing her to spread to give me room. With my hands on her hips, I hold her in place.

"On the side of the road? Going for something extra-kinky now, are we?" She's teasing me, and I know that if I laid her back, she'd let me fuck her tight little pussy right here, right now. But I can hear the hurt in her voice, her usual spark lacking.

"Brat, that's not what I'm doing. Or at least not yet.

First, we need to talk. And not snarky fun this time. Serious and real. You in?" I ask, but I'm not going to let her say no. This conversation is happening.

"Ooh, cocky bastard is back, is he?" she tries once more, her eyes begging me not to do this. But I think she doesn't quite know where I'm going with this conversation and that's why she doesn't want to give in to having it.

"Stop. I'm not fucking around, Norma." Her eyes flash fire at me, and if looks could kill, I'd probably be dead where I stand. I reach up, pulling the scarf from its near-constant place around her head, and move to use it in the other place it usually resides. "Put your hands together."

She sighs but gives me her wrists, and I loosely tie them together. She could get out, same as always, but the symbolism of her letting me be in control is more powerful in this moment than ever before. I know she's kicking and screaming against this conversation on the inside, but it's what we need, a dose of seriousness in the midst of all our usual play.

She rests her bound hands in her lap, but I lift them, placing them behind my neck and crowding into her, face to face. The bumper of her car presses against my knees, but I need to be close to her for this. "Listen to me. I detested the idea of needing a tutor in the first place. Thought the whole secret girlfriend shit was stupid as fuck. And then I walked in that library and you busted my balls like no one ever has, completely unimpressed with me and my shit." Her eyes drift down, but they snap back up at my next words.

"I *liked* it. Liked your sass and your backbone and the way you can use words like knives but only do it in a fun way. When you sparred with me verbally, it made me feel like I was a worthy opponent. And fucking you, here, there, and everywhere, has been hotter than I could've ever imagined. Being the first man to be inside you is an honor I will always cherish."

I can see the tears glistening in her eyes, but strong-willed woman that she is, she holds them back along with any verbal indication of what she's thinking. My girl who usually won't shut up isn't saying a word.

"I wasn't looking for any of this, but I found it. I found you, and I will shout from any damn mountaintop you want me to that we're together. I'll meet your brother and your parents. We can walk hand-in-fucking-hand along the field at half-time if you want. Tattoo your name on my ass in that fancy scripty font girls like . . ." I'm running out of grand gestures to list so I thank God when she laughs.

She sniffs a bit, her nose runny from the unshed tears, but the smile is back on her face and her laughter is like a balm. "No tattoos, hero. But the rest sounds pretty stellar." She sobers, though this time, it feels like she's with me, no walls and unfiltered. "I'm sorry, Zach. Truly. I wasn't looking for this either, and I don't exactly have the best track record with guys hanging around. Sure, I'm fun to be *friends* with and have liter-ally been told that I'm great in small doses, so I just keep waiting for the other shoe to drop, for you to figure out that I'm not worth the effort to hang around. I'm not easy and I know that, and you're . . . you. You could have any girl on campus you want, so why would you be with me?"

The admission seems like it hurts her to say, and I realize that for all her strength, my Brat is a softie underneath, scared to get hurt just like the rest of us. It's a surprising revelation, though I guess it shouldn't be. She's human and victim to the same insecurities we all are. She just hides hers a bit better than most, deeper in the shadows of her heart, not one to show her weak spots.

Wanting to soften it for her, I let just a hint of tease into my voice and let her see the sparkle in my eye as I say, "Let's be clear. I'm a fucking football god. I could have virtually any woman I want, period. Not just on campus." She rolls her eyes, and I continue as I grasp her chin, forcing her to see the truth in my words. "And I chose you. I choose you every damn day, Brat. You keep me on my toes, keep things interesting. Choose me back."

She chuckles a bit. "Fine. I choose you too." The words are full of humor, like she's giving in to something silly, but I can hear the honesty in them, feel the weight of them, and I know they mean just as much to her as they do to me.

She looks around us, the dark night pressing in like a blanket, stars above us twinkling like fairy lights, and down below, the occasional headlight or taillight passing on the main road. "So . . . you said you like to keep things interesting, right?"

I can hear the dare in her voice, the challenge to fuck

her right here on the side of the road where anyone might drive by or even someone on the main road might notice if they looked up at just the right time.

I yank her from the hood of the car, her hands scrambling to grab at me, but they're uselessly tossed over my head still and she can't get purchase. I grab her head in my hand, tilting it the way I want and taking her mouth in a hot, passionate kiss. She moans into me, and I swallow every sound, wanting to keep not just her sass but her submission as my own.

I step back, lifting her hands over my head and spinning her in place. A press to her back has her bending over the hood, ass presented perfectly for me and her hands reaching toward the windshield. Our conversation . . . the truth and the heaviness ride me, and I need to claim her, make sure she fucking knows that we're in this together. That she's mine.

She is mine. See those hands? They aren't letting go of that knot. And she has just as tight a grip on my fucking heart. She's mine, and I'm fucking hers.

I rip her skirt up, exposing her ass to the night air. Her panties are soaked, the silky white covering of her pussy almost sheer with her arousal. My already rock-hard cock throbs in my pants, and I'm tempted to take her right here. But this is about showing her more, showing her something new, and I lick the fabric, her breath catching as I tease her clit through her panties. "Zach . . . oh, God."

I reach up, hooking my thumbs in her panties and rolling them down her thighs. Folding them in half, I tuck them in my pocket, for a half-second wondering if Norma knows I've kept four other pairs from special encounters. Regardless, the scent of her arousal hits me in the face, my mouth watering as I start licking and sucking on her sweet folds and silky soft lips.

"Spread wide for me." She steps her heeled feet wider without the restriction of the skirt, and I growl, grabbing a handful of her ass in each hand.

She cries out, pressing into my palms. "Please, Zach. Just fuck me. I need you."

I lay one long lick to her pussy, starting with a flick of my tongue against her clit and then through her folds, up to the puckered rosebud of her asshole, where I swirl my tongue. She bucks, and I know it's her first time being touched there. The thought makes me want to take her virgin ass too. But not tonight.

I pull my sweatpants down, letting my cock spring free to tease along her slit, getting myself coated in her juices. "Goddamn, you're fucking soaked. So sexy. Tell me, Norma. Use those damn words of yours and tell me what you want."

She squirms, trying to impale herself on my cock, and I press her hips to the hood, not letting her take it without saying it. She lets out a cute kitten growl of frustration and finally gives in. "Fuck me. Slide that awesome fucking cock of yours into my pussy and make me come."

At her order, I do it, slamming balls-deep in one stroke and going full-power from the get-go with no time for her to adjust. My hips slap against her ass, and she bucks, trying to fuck me back. I grab her hips, helping her move. It's hard, rough, and passionately violent. It's exactly what we need after all the truth of the night.

But I know there's more.

"That's not all though, is it, Brat? You don't just want me to fuck you. You want me to fuck you in the shadows of the library, in the dark of night on the side of the road. Where someone might see you being my fucking dirty girl, getting plowed so hard and raw you have to fight back the screams. You want me to fuck you with your hands tied up in the silk scarves I know you only wear as a way of wordlessly asking me to do this to you. This is what you want, to be my tied up, submissive fucktoy, and you like that someone might see you getting filled by your arrogant bastard jock boyfriend." Every word of my filthy talk is true, and I pound home each one with another powerful stroke inside her.

She's trembling beneath me, her pussy a mess of her cream and my pre-cum as she gasps out with every thrust. "Ohh . . . Zach . . . I'm gonna come." Her voice is getting higher-pitched and louder. In the shadow of night, it carries, and I love that down the street, someone might be letting their dog out for the night for a bedtime piss and instead, they hear us.

"Not until you say it, Brat. Tell me I'm right," I grunt, "look over there at those headlights, any one of which could be someone who sees us." I tangle my fingers in her hair, holding her head to the side so that her eyes can lock on the vehicles driving by, not exactly close, but close enough to feel taboo. I grind deep inside her, giving her time to see a few headlights pass.

She cries out at the change in sensation, and faster than I'd meant for her to, she falls off the edge. Shudders rack her body and her pussy squeezes me like a vice, but mixed in with her shouts of pleasure, she gives me what I demanded. "Yes . . . it's all true. Fuck me anywhere, even if we might get caught. I just want you, Zach!"

Her admission and naughty words are my undoing, and I follow her over, coming hard and groaning loudly as rope after rope of my cum fill her tight pussy.

Panting as we both come back to earth, I help her stand up. Turning her head toward me, I kiss her, the smack of our lips replacing the smack of my hips against her. "Fuck, Brat. That was amazing."

I let my cock leave her body, instantly feeling the loss, and she whimpers a bit too. I spin her, untying her scarf and handing it back to her. "Now what? You ready to head home? It's pretty late." I look up to the pitch-black sky and then at all the shadows surrounding us.

Norma smirks and then sasses, "You promised me door number one and door number two earlier."

I have no idea what she's talking about, my brain pretty much fried after sex and our conversation. I lift my brows in question.

"Earlier, you said door number two was dinner. But door number one was something else." She sticks her tongue out, licking her red lips, and like a flash, I remember. I told her she could suck me off and leave that red lipstick all over me. The lipstick is still there, must be some of that fancy kiss-proof shit girls wear, but I'm all for trying to get it to smudge.

"You gonna clean me off, Brat? Suck me off right here?" I ask, letting my thumb trace the edge of her lip.

She bites her lip, narrowly missing the pad of my finger, and smiles naughtily. "Nope. Get in the car, asshole."

"Asshole? Is that what you call guys when they make you come like a damn freight train against the hood of your very practical and reliable fancy car?" I tease, liking that we're back to this space between us.

"Apparently, but you'd be the only one who'd know." She smirks, and I hear the compliment in the words. That I'm the one she chose to give her virginity to, and as much as she may give me a hard time, we both know that was a big deal. That *we* are a big deal.

Norma drives for a few minutes, looping down toward the main road but then pulling off at an exit and parking again, just off the highway on the shoulder. And then she looks at me with a devilish grin.

"Here?" I ask, surprised. "We're literally on the side of the road."

"Yep," she says, letting the word pop her lips. "I watched the cars like you told me to. There's only a few going by, no traffic or anything."

I turn and look behind us. "What if a cop stops?"

She widens her eyes, looking innocent as hell, but I know it's a front because my Brat is anything but innocent. "Guess you'll have to keep your eyes open and keep watch."

I grin back, knowing we're doing this. I gesture to my cock. "All yours, Brat. Show me what you've got."

She looks in the rearview mirror one time and then lies over the console. I help her slip my dick free of my pants and then she breathes on me. I'm inpatient, ready for this in a way I don't know that I've ever been. Sure, she's sucked me in dim corners at the library, but this seems riskier somehow. I fucking love it.

She laps at my tip, swirling her tongue around it before taking me into her mouth. "Fuck, Norma, I love it when you do that."

She hums against me and goes deeper. I spread my legs to give her room to work, letting one of my hands drift into her hair and the other down to hold myself straight up for her, giving her a better angle. She dives in, covering my whole cock with the wet warmth of her mouth, and she begins to suck me, each stroke up and down better than the one before as she takes me higher and higher as she goes deeper and deeper.

I groan, trying but failing to keep my hips still. I buck into her mouth, already about to come. I glance in the mirror and see headlights coming up behind us.

"Don't stop, don't stop," I beg. Norma thinks I'm talking to her, and maybe I am, but I'm also praying that car doesn't stop and get a view of my girl's mouth full of my cock. Because if someone tapped on the glass right now, I don't know that I could let her pull off me. I need this, so close . . .

The car whooshes by in a whir of speed, and I come, filling her mouth as I cry out, my hand gripping the headrest behind me as I lift my hips so that my Brat can take every bit of me. "Fuck . . . yeah!"

When she sits back up, there's no red on my cock and her lips look just as pristine as they did when I picked her up. But we're both undone from the night.

We might not have studied for shit, but I feel like I got a great big lesson in all things Norma Jean Blackstone.

CHAPTER 12

ZACH

I don't think I've ever enjoyed college this much. On the football field, the Ravens are undefeated. Now the pursuit is for the conference championship, and if we can do that, the sky's the limit.

But it's not just football. The weeks that I've been studying with Norma have been . . . something. My little Brat makes studying at least tolerable, and while Milton isn't going to be on my Kindle for away games anytime soon, I'm doing well.

How well? Well, enough that my weekly essays are coming back with Bs and even an A on one of them. I've got a B in English already, and if I stick with it, I might even pull out a B-plus. Hell, might set my sights on an A with her help.

Part of it, of course, is her sassy mouth. I can't make a single statement in our discussions without having to justify it. Norma knows just how to press my buttons too, and while the acid that used to coat her tongue isn't there any longer, she still gives as good as takes, verbally speaking. And she doesn't let me just skirt by easily. When we're in study mode, I can't even seduce her . . . most of the time.

Not that we don't seduce each other. She's even taken the lead sometimes, and the more she does it, the more it thrills me. I'll never forget the time she gave me a surreptitious hand job in the middle of the library for getting an 'A' on that essay, her face impassive as she talked about temptation and Satan's role as an anti-hero. Meanwhile, underneath the table, her hand was milking my cock, and I had to untuck my shirt to make it back to the dorm without giving myself away after our 'tutoring.'

Simply put, sex with her is awesome. Every time is more fun than the last, and we're constantly one-upping the other with how intense and fun we can make it.

And that's what makes Norma different. She's . . . special. It can work.

The thought is undeniable as I jog out onto the field for Homecoming. The Ravens have homecoming relatively late, and this year, it's an important game. If we win this, we're nearly locked for the conference championship in three weeks. The only games we've got left are against teams we should beat. All we have to do is play our game the way I know we can.

"How're you feeling, Son?" Coach Jefferson asks as we wait on the sidelines for the senior captains to do the coin toss. "We're on TV today. You know some scouts are going to be watching, maybe here but definitely later." He scans the crowd, like he could spot a scout at this distance.

"Don't sweat it, Coach. There will be plenty of high-lights to choose from for my reel," I promise him. "You just get ready for the Gatorade bath."

I glance up in the stands, but I can't see Norma in the mass of tens of thousands of fans here to see the Ravens take on the Bulldogs. But I know she's here, wearing a team shirt to support me and ready to cheer like crazy.

I put it out of my mind as we take the field, needing my brain to focus because it's time to work. We run the first three plays just as Coach scripted, burning the Bulldogs for two good passes before we get stuffed on the third play.

Looking over at the sidelines, I watch as Jake gets the play from Coach, sending in the signals. "What the fuck?" I mutter.

Settling into the huddle, I call the play. "Trips left Camelot, Rodeo 82 Ninja on three."

"Are you out of your fucking mind, man?" Will Franklin, my left tackle and our senior captain, asks. "They're stacking the box."

"Coach called it. Now run it," I say, putting that tone in my voice that says cut the bullshit. Will shuts his mouth, and the huddle breaks, but as soon as I settle into the shotgun, I know Will is right. This makes no sense.

They're coming at me hard. They have to, so why this play? I'm only going to have five guys protecting me. Everyone else is going deep. This is a play we normally only run in long ball, no-pressure situations. Now, I'm not afraid to stand in the pocket. Every quarterback's expected to take a shot from time to time, but this is suicide. Tugging on my facemask, I make a decision to overrule coach and audible it.

It's a risk. The crowd's going nuts and I'm not sure anyone can hear me, but I have to trust that my teammates can. The ball snaps, and I roll right, avoiding the manic Bulldog rush as I look for an opening.

Nothing. I've got half a second to make a decision to either run or pass when I see it. Not even breaking stride, I laser the ball downfield to our tight end, who takes it the rest of the way in for a touchdown.

Jogging off the field, Coach Buckley gives me a pat on the shoulder. "Great call, Son! Can't argue with a touchdown."

"No problem, but why did you send in that play?"

Before he can answer, Coach Jefferson calls him over and I can't get an answer. For the rest of the first half, though, I keep getting strange signals from the sidelines, and more than once, I'm changing plays at the line. When we go in for halftime, we're up, but it's not by what we wanted.

"What the hell's going on out there, Zach?" Coach Buckley asks as the locker room door closes. "You keep changing the play at the line out there."

"Coach, I'd call them like you send them in, but the signals aren't making any sense with what's happening on the field!" I growl, trying to keep my voice low.

Coach is a good guy, and I learned to never disrespect a Coach where others can hear you. "I swear, every time we're in a position to run for the first down or work the short routes and sidelines, you're wanting me to stand back there and throw bombs!"

Buckley stops, tilting his head. "What the hell do you mean? I know they're trying to pressure you."

"Then why do you keep sending in plays for me to sit in the pocket? That's what Jake's signaling."

Coach stops and looks at Jake, who's trying to look innocent and failing. "Jake? What the fuck are you doing out there?"

And though my attention laser-focuses on Jake, I'm aware that there is a whole room full of guys watching and listening to the exchange now.

Jake seems to realize the same thing, looking around at the team with his hands held wide. He hems and haws. "I don't know what you mean, Coach. I just send in what you tell me to. But if Zach can't handle it, that's on him. You know I'll step in for the team if he's pussing out."

Coach's eyes narrow, looking between the two of us. "I don't have time to deal with this shit. Second half, I'll send in the signals myself. Jake, sideline. Zach, win the damn game."

He walks off, and I turn to Jake, shaking my head. "You really are a snake, aren't you? You trying to get me fucking injured out there?"

Jake looks at me, his jaw clenching as he stares at me.

"The team would be better with me out there. I should be the one getting the headlines, goddammit."

"Don't fucking stab your own teammate in the back. That just shows why you *shouldn't* be out there," I growl.

I should say a lot more. Hell, I'm *this close* to beating the shit out of him. But I have no proof he's done it on purpose. It's obvious now that he did, but he'll weasel his fucking way out of it with Coach and I'll be the one talking shit like a crybaby. But with the whole team watching, this isn't about the coaches. Every man in this room knows in his gut that Jake just tried to have me sacked on the line so that he could get some grass time.

And that shit doesn't fly. Not with any team, but especially not with the Ravens. The circle of guys gathers closer and I think Jake can see the sea of fury encroaching.

He pushes past one of the smaller guys and makes a break for the locker room door. "Whatever. Glory hound," Jake says, turning away.

I look around at the guys, who are waiting for my signal on how we want to handle Jake's breech of the football code. "Fuck that asshole. We have a game to win." Will takes over the pep talk from there, and we run back out, ready to rock.

The second half is a total turnaround. With Coach Buckley running the signals directly to me, our offense clicks on all cylinders, and we unleash hell on the Bulldogs. We're so far ahead, the Bulldogs don't have a chance at recovering, so Coach pulls me out and lets

Jake get some field time . . . and to ensure I don't end up with some stupid injury that didn't have to happen.

I'm pretty satisfied when the whole defensive line seems to instantly falter and a lineman gets through to Jake, sacking him to the grass. The same thing happens on the next play. Jake's time on the field is basically useless as he keeps eating the turf. We keep the Bulldogs from making any headway, but the team sacrifices gaining any ourselves.

It's still a shootout, though, and as the guys pile off the field, they all give me high-fives. Will stops, pressing his helmet to my forehead and talking low. "Ravens don't put up with that shit. But you need to let it go now. We fought your battle for you so that you wouldn't fuck up your future. You got me?"

I nod back, the significance of what he's saying sinking in. "Thanks, man. You didn't have to do that. But thanks."

He grins and gives me a big wink before letting out a big whooping yell. "We were gonna win, no matter what! Ravens forever! Let's hear it for my man, Zach!"

And like the bottle's been uncorked, the excitement bubbles over. Everyone's congratulating me, and Coach Jefferson doesn't even wait until we're back in the locker room to toss me the game ball in front of the stands. "You earned it, Son. Damn fine job today!"

I smile and nod, telling him thanks. The team lines up near the student section for the Alma Mater, but before we're even started, I see Jake turn and storm off the field. Whatever. I bet Coach will chew his ass for it, and in the future, I'm going to insist he doesn't relay the calls. He's got a knife, and it's pointed right at my back. Luckily, the rest of the guys have me and I have them.

The music plays on, and it's a great feeling to stand here with my team, knowing we're playing our best season ever. But regardless of how much everyone might be pounding my shoulders and congratulating me, I should be enjoying this whole thing with my girl.

Yes, *my* girl.

I look out into the crowd, and at that moment, I see her in the stands. I wave to her, feeling slightly stupid, but when she waves back, it feels good to know I've been playing a great game in front of her.

Suddenly, the guys all crowd around and in one big mosh pit of craziness, I'm shuffled to the locker room amid the celebration. I manage to poke my head up above the mass and yell, "Norma, meet me by the locker room!" I think I see her nod before I'm carried away.

CHAPTER 13

*T*he game is amazing! I'm kind of ashamed to admit it, but I've never been to one of our college games. Not until Zach. Sure, I've seen them on television, and I went to a few of the important games in high school, but it's nothing like the rush of a college Homecoming game. The stands are a sea of black and gold for the Ravens and red and white for the Bulldogs. There's an undulating energy to the crowd, everyone cheering and booing in unison as the teams battle it out on the field. And watching Zach play the game that he loves, I'm suddenly struck with understanding why he loves it so much.

Somewhere after half-time, I hear my name being shouted from the stands below me. I scan the crowd and see Erica waving at me. I smile and wave back and she starts to work her way up to me. Luckily, the couple sitting next to me seem to be on a bathroom break and Erica sneaks into one of their seats for a minute.

"Hey, girl! Never thought I'd see you at a game! What

do you think?" she asks excitedly. I grin, enjoying seeing my usually serious and hard-pressing boss a bit crazy. Her hair is pulled up in a big cheerleader bow that's almost as big as my palm and she has logoed eye black on her cheeks, her right proclaiming *Ravens* and her left *#1*. She's also wearing a team shirt and has a pompom on a stick. She's a fangirl, which surprises me somehow.

"I love it! Look at you . . . you're totally a football groupie!" I say with a laugh.

She laughs and shakes her head. "No, more like a super fan. I'm not a dick-hopping groupie when I've got a good one of my own." She leans close and points back down where she was sitting, where as if he sensed she was talking about him, a good-looking guy turns around and smiles at Erica. She gives him a little finger waggle and he laughs before going back to watching the game. "So, you here for Zach?"

I nod. "Yeah, I'm meeting him after the game for some HoCo team party. Supposed to be fun, but I'm nervous." The admission is truer than I'd like to admit. What we have together is awesome, but introducing me to his team feels like it's on par with me introducing him to Liam. Major.

"Ooh, have fun! That's probably a big deal to take someone as your girl, not your flavor of the week. Seems like maybe I was wrong about Zach and you. Maybe you do have a magic pussy that can tame the wildest of manwhores? You'll have to tell me all your secrets." She says it jokingly, and I realize she's probably mildly drunk and not filtering, but it's still a bit of a sting.

"Oh, yeah, pussy whipped him right into shape," I joke, playing off the pseudo-compliment.

But she doesn't stop, "Girl, I would've bet money that you would've barely been able to tutor him successfully, much less turn his eye. Not because you're not gorgeous, because I mean, have you seen you?" She grins loopily. "But he's just . . . Zach Knight, Quarterback Extraordinaire. He could have pussy twenty-four, seven if he wanted."

She's not wrong. Hell, I basically said as much to Zach. But he reassured me that he wants only me and I believed him. I do believe him. But it's hard to remember that when Erica is verbalizing the same insecurities that I already have.

"Yeah, good thing he's got mine then, I suppose," I say with a bit of a bite. Luckily, the couple returns from the bathroom right then and saves me from any more of Erica's drunken disbelief at my relationship with Zach.

She waves and heads back to her guy, magically not stumbling on a single step. So maybe not that drunk. Just enough to insult me, apparently. I give a moment's thought that maybe she's more sour-grapes-jealous than surprised. Her whole outfit and enthusiasm could be school spirit, but right now, if someone told me she was a bit more toward the groupie end of the spectrum, I wouldn't be surprised.

I try to let that temper the effect of her words, to let them go and enjoy the game.

And as the third quarter turns to the fourth, I'm pretty ensnared in the game again, even when Zach gets pulled to the sidelines for a bit. From listening to the fans around me, I figure out that the Coach is letting Jake get some time, but once Zach is off the field, I quit watching the game and instead watch him on the sideline.

And when we win, pandemonium breaks out and the hugely wide grin on Zach's face is beautiful. When he looks up to find me in the stands and we wave back and forth, it feels like he invited me in to this special moment, shared his joy with me across the distance separating us. I see his head pop up as the crowd pushes toward the end zone and see him pointing and mouthing, "Meet me outside the locker room." I nod back, but he's gone in the mob.

I wait for the stands to clear a bit before working my way down and out, following the throng of people before turning off to head toward the locker room hall-way. Down here, the mass clears a bit, giving me a clear sightline to Zach leaning up against the wall. I smile at the sight of him, freshly-showered damp hair mussed, a black T-shirt stretched tight across the muscles of his chest, and what are quickly becoming my favorite grey sweatpants. I'm so busy checking him out that it takes me a minute to realize that he's smiling while talking to someone.

I follow his gaze to see a blonde Barbie-looking girl standing in front of him. She's looking up at him with a flirty smile, twirling a lock of hair around a manicured finger as she chats back. I don't need to hear the words to know that she's basically propositioning him because her every intention is being broadcast absolutely one hundred percent loud and clear.

A stab of jealousy, hot and bitter, punches me in the gut. I'm torn. There's the one side of me that wants to haul ass over there and basically mark my damn territory, push Blonde Barbie the fuck away from what's mine. But I'm pissed at myself to admit there's a tiny wiggle deep in my brain that says I should've known. Like Erica said, Zach has always been a bit of a manwhore, and while he's been nothing but gentlemanly with me, at the least, maybe he'd prefer someone easier, less prickly and snarky?

And just like always, when I get a bit out of sorts, I react by going full-throttle. I basically stomp my way over to Zach, but about halfway there, he turns and sees my incoming fury. His smile just pisses me off more.

My voice is stone-cold as I get to his side. "Zach."

He puts an arm around my shoulder, pulling me to his side. "Hey, Brat! Been looking for you."

My eyes shoot daggers and his grin grows. I swear he even chuckles a bit. "Norma, this is Beth. Beth, this is Norma. Beth is 'like my biggest fan ever!" he says, obviously mimicking Beth's voice. "Norma is my girlfriend."

I watch Beth's eyes widen and then narrow as she very obviously looks me up and down, judging my worthiness. My inner bitch is yelling *you can fuck right off, Beth*. And though every instinct is telling me to verbally slice and dice her, I know that's not the best move here and would only make me seem bitchy and insecure. And while that's probably true, at least to some degree, I force myself to calm down and take the high road.

I channel the cool demeanor I've seen my dad give to

opposing business forces, the one my mom has given to waitresses the world over when they flirt with my dad in front of her, and give Beth the smile that says I consider her less than a worthy opponent. That I consider her inconsequential, less than a footnote to the highlights of my day. "Nice to meet you, Beth."

She smiles back, just as fake as the boobs pressed up damn near to her chin, but she doesn't address me, instead keeping her lasers locked on Zach. "Oh, your *girlfriend*. Right. Well, I guess I'd better be going for now then. See you *later*, Zach." Every word is designed to sound like she's covering some big secret between the two of them. She blows a smacking kiss at the air, aimed right for his mouth, then pivots and sashays away, her hips exaggeratedly swinging right and left.

To his credit, Zach doesn't even watch her go. Instead, he steps in front of me, caging me in his arms and pressing me back against the wall. "You surprise the hell out of me, Brat."

I look away, refusing to meet his eyes, but he tilts my chin, forcing me to.

"You are so fucking jealous. You were strutting over here like some sexy Valkyrie about to demolish that girl. I'll admit, I was a little excited to see you trash talk her, reduce her to a crying puddle on the ground, because I know that sharp tongue of yours could do it in a heart-beat. But instead, you went all responsible and mature on me, like you knew that I was yours and wasn't going anywhere, not when I have something as special as you in the palm of my hand."

To emphasize his words, he lets one hand cup my ass, squeezing hard enough to make me gasp. "I had a moment where I almost made some vulgar joke about her fake tits or bottle blonde, but when they make it that easy, it's almost a pity to use it. Lowest common denominator shit," I admit. "And it hit me that I was jealous because of the possibility, not that you were actually doing anything or even considering it. And that opportunity is always out there. I don't want to be *that* girl. You don't deserve for me to be that way because you've given me no reason to mistrust you. It's just my own fears and doubts."

"So don't be scared. Don't doubt me, and sure as fuck don't doubt us. Because it's me and you, Brat." His words are serious, solemn like a promise. "You need to do some territory marking to get it out of your system? Because I could be down for that." He grins, like it's a joke, but leans close to whisper in my left ear, "You need to leave a mark on my neck before we go to this party?" He tilts his head, almost like he's deferring to me, and the expanse of his neck is right there, so warm. I can see his heartbeat racing, so I lean forward to lick it and then lay a soft kiss, letting the beat pulse against my lips.

I move to his ear, whispering back. "I don't need to mark your neck like I've got something to prove to everyone else. They can fuck off. All I care is that you're marked here . . ." I lay my palm against his heart, and my other against my own. "And so am I."

His breath hitches. I'm holding mine. The moment stretches, and I can almost taste the three little words in the pregnant pause between us, neither of us willing to say them yet but both acknowledging that they're true. That this is real. So fucking real.

"Goddammit, Brat. That's the sexiest thing anyone's ever said to me. Come on." He grabs my hand, dragging me down the hallway and around under the bleachers until we find a deserted corner in Section 67.

He pulls me close and crushes my lips in a fierce kiss. I melt against him as we descend deeper into the shadows, out of view, though I can still hear people moving through the stadium a little bit away.

He nibbles on my ear, making my thoughts and our previous conversation scatter like the wind. "You were a god out there today."

He cups my breast, teasing the stiff nipple and pinching me lightly. "Did you like watching me play?"

I slip my hand inside his sweatpants, grasping his thick cock and stroking it to rock hardness while he tugs at the button of my jeans, undoing them and rubbing at my drenched panties. "What do you think? I wanted to—"

"Hey, Louie, you gettin' the brooms?"

We freeze as a voice calls out, seemingly just outside the alcove we're hiding in. It's one of the stadium workers, probably getting everything together for cleanup.

"Don't move," Zach whispers, but he spins me, shoving my jeans and panties down. Suddenly, his cock is right at my entrance, and without notice, he thrusts inside me. He clamps his hand over my mouth to stifle the moan he knows is coming when he fills me.

The stadium worker is oblivious as Zach starts stroking in and out of my pussy, my body clenching, already on the edge from the feel of him inside me and the thrill of what we're doing. It's impossible to be totally quiet, the soft wet sounds of my pussy taking his every plunge seeming to echo around us, but no one peeks around the corner to catch us.

I turn my head, my eyes swimming with lust . . . and something more, needing to see it reflected in Zach's eyes. His blue eyes lock onto mine and he nods. There wasn't a question, but I know he's telling me that he feels this too. My body ramps up, tighter and higher, my lips pressed together behind his palm.

We hear the stadium worker talking, his voice getting quieter and quieter as he walks away from our hiding spot. Zach growls in my ear, "That was so hot, wasn't it, Brat? You wanted to come all over my cock knowing someone else might hear you, might see you getting fucked under the bleachers by your football god."

I nod as he hammers into me, whimpering as I try to hold back my cries.

But he's not done. He rumbles, "You might be evolved . . . not need to mark me up, but I'm just a cocky bastard caveman. I know I have you here," he says, taking the risk of removing his hand from my mouth to place it against my chest. His thumb flicks at my nipple, but I know he means my heart. "But I need to mark you inside and out because you're fucking mine, Brat."

His other hand grips my hip tightly, dimpling in the skin,

and I know it'll leave bruises. I welcome them, want his mark if that's what he wants. Hell, I'm rethinking my previous stance on leaving a hickie on his neck because being in his rough grasp is heaven.

I hear footsteps, but it's too late. There's no stopping us now.

Zach pounds into me, hips slapping my ass with every thrust like he's given up on being quiet. I tighten my pussy around him, and it's enough to send us both over. I clench my teeth, and a glance over my shoulder shows Zach's jaw clamped tight too, both of us trying to contain our cries as our orgasms rock our bodies. I feel him fill my pussy with his cum, and I milk him, wanting every last drop.

We sag as Zach pulls out, breaths panting and happy smiles on both of our faces. We got away with it. Again.

"God, you make me so fucking crazy. That was hot," I whisper, tugging my panties up. "I couldn't believe you kept going."

Zach steps closer, stopping me from pulling my jeans up though his sweatpants are already back in place. He cups my pussy through my wet panties. "I couldn't stop. Didn't care if we got caught as long as I got this sweet pussy. And now you're marked . . . inside." He touches my chest like he did before and then grinds his palm against my lips. He smirks. "And out." He smacks my ass over the sensitive area he'd been gripping, the sound echoing around us as it bounces off the metal bleachers.

I grin back, liking the way he thinks. "So caveman, Zach," I tease.

But he knows. "Just the way you like me, Brat. Now let's get to the after-party. The guys are all dying to meet you. Fair warning, I might've talked about you . . . a lot."

I blush. "Oh, God, what did you tell them?"

I swear Zach blushes a bit, but surely, that's just a trick of the lights. "Just that you're bratty and prickly and can cut just about anyone down in under ten words. You probably need to get your game face on because they're ready for you to wow them."

"Shit, no pressure or anything though, right? And you tell me this now? After fucking my brains out, where I have no hope of forming coherent sentences."

He winks at me. "Well, I had to give them a fair shot. It's like a head start for them, because they'll need it against you. I might've also told them that you're my girlfriend, and now they want to meet the 'witch who cursed me', though I think that's supposed to be a dig on me more than any commentary on your spellcasting abilities."

I sigh, looking heavenward as though I need strength. "Well, let's do this then," I say, sounding like I'm dreading every bit of this. I'm actually excited to hear that Zach's been talking about me with his team. And nervous to meet them because these are Zach's people. And meeting someone's people is a big deal.

Zach looks down at me like he knows every thought that just ran through my mind. Hell, he probably actually does. "You'll do fine, Norma. They're gonna love you and you're gonna love them."

I swear I thought he was about to say his team would love me like he does, but the words didn't come. I'm not disappointed though. I feel like we're there, just hovering on that edge of admission, and it's a sweet moment of anticipation, knowing that it's coming. For him and for me.

CHAPTER 14

NORMA

*D*ear Diary,

The past weeks have been amazing! I feel like Zach and I have reached a place of excited-comfort. Yeah, I know those two words are pretty much the antithesis of each other, but it's the best way I know to describe where we are.

I guess I never realized that my lack of positive romantic relationships had done a bit of a number on me. That maybe my jump to sarcasm was preemptively defensive. But with Zach, there's no need to be constantly on alert. And we've had some rather insightful, deep conversations, acknowledging feelings that I usually hide behind snark, and even building some bridges over my insecurities. My trust that he's going to hang through the challenge of being with me hasn't dulled my sharp tongue, though. But it's . . . evolved? I guess that's the right word. We zing each other but then bust up laughing, high-fiving as we say 'good one' or lobbing a verbal softball to let the other slam-dunk it. It's easy, fun, and . . . comfortable.

But it's not all prose and slam poetry, which though they are thrilling, are nothing compared to our sex life. I almost can't believe that I can actually say that . . . my sex life! From virgin to fuck-me-anywhere-and-anytime in a whiplash of 'Oh, God. Yeah!' Definitely exciting.

Somehow all mixed together, though, Zach and I have reached a place I wasn't sure I'd ever get to. Excited comfort. Him, my cocky jock who puts up with my prickliness and calls me on my sass. Me, his mouthy brat who challenges him to use his brain and supports his dreams on and off the football field.

I'VE GOT BIG PLANS TODAY.

Big, responsible plans that include such titillating endeavors as writing a three-hundred-word article on the new smoothie cart in the quad, studying vocabulary words for biology, and reading the last section of *Paradise Lost* for my *study* session with Zach tonight. But all of that has to wait until I finish my cup of coffee and take a shower because I need the wake-me-up to get rolling on my list that doesn't sound bad but will definitely keep me busy while Zach hits the weight room with the team this afternoon.

I'm mid-caffeine fix when my phone rings. Recognizing Madonna's "Papa Don't Preach" and hoping that my dad will listen to the prayer, I answer.

"Hey, Daddy!" Somehow, my voice usually reverts to a younger version of myself when I talk to him.

"Norma Jean. There's my little ladybug. How're you doing, baby?" He regresses to the childhood nicknames he's always called me too. Secretly, I love it, though I sometimes tease him that I'm not quite as small as a 'red-headed ladybug' anymore. He always winks and tells me that to him, I'll always be his ladybug.

"Doing great, working hard at the paper and keeping my grades up in all my classes. The usual. How're you doing? What are you and Mom up to?" I ask, knowing that these are just pleasant niceties until we get to the meat of the conversation. I love my dad, and he loves me, but he's a dedicated businessman through and through, not one for small talk, though I know he keeps up with what's going on in my life through Mom.

"Good to hear. Keep working, Norma Jean, and you're going to be running *The Chronicle* by your senior year." I smile at his certainty, knowing that's my hope too. "Your mother is industrious, as always. I believe her current charity du jour is something about rescue dogs? Oh, greyhounds . . . that's it, rehoming race dogs. She actually mentioned bringing one home, if you can imagine, but when I reminded her that dogs tend to make her sneeze, she doubled down on finding twice as many their forever homes. I think that's a win-win, for me and the dogs."

I laugh. Though I've already heard the story from Mom, it's interesting to hear my dad's take on the conversation. My mom's version featured him grumping that she 'wasn't bringing an animal that had never known grass to live in a penthouse apartment because it'd be torture for the poor critter even if it was luxury to them.' That's my dad . . . steel exterior that he shows to the world, and the softest teddy bear center he shows to my mom, and sometimes to me.

"Well, good for them . . . and for you, then." I wait, knowing he'll get around to his real reason for the call if I give him the opening.

"I wanted to see if you're available for lunch today. It's a business thing and my associate is bringing his son, so I need my daughter there to represent the family name." His tone has switched to a more clipped professional cadence and I can vaguely hear papers flipping in the background.

"Dad, I've got to study today. Maybe some other time?" I say, hoping for the out. I'd love to have lunch with him, but a dry business lunch sounds ridiculously boring and irresponsible with my limited time.

"Norma. I'd like to have lunch with my only daughter today. It'll help me out, and my associate will be grateful to have someone age-appropriate to engage with his son while we talk business. Please." He's not asking, he's telling me that I'm doing this.

"Fine, Dad. What time and where?" I say, making sure the eyeroll is audible in the sigh I add to the words.

After a quick breakdown of lunch expectations, we hang up.

So much for a useful day of productivity.

"Ladybug, so good of you to come on such short

notice," Dad says as he opens the door. It's his version of acknowledging that this is a big ask and saying thank you.

I nod. "Of course." As I come in, I see that Mom has had the foyer painted again . . . or at least I think it was blue last time I was here. Truth be told, I don't come to this property often. It's right downtown, near Blackstone Industries and close to campus, but Dad's rarely here. He spends most of his time in luxury hotel rooms on his innumerable business trips. And Mom prefers to stay in the 'country house' just outside the city limits. Yes, that's actually what they call it. Admittedly, I live in a strange world, straddling the ridiculous wealth I grew up in and my own rather middle-class current situation, but even that is funded by my parents. But one day, I'll be self-sufficient. I can't wait to have a little studio apartment of my very own with my name on the lease. Maybe an odd dream for a 'spoiled little rich girl' but it's the truth. I want to make it on my own. Just like my dad. Just like my brother.

"Come, let me introduce you." I follow my dad into the living room where two men stand up as I enter. They're obviously father and son, looking like a time-progression photo of the same person. "Norma, this is my friend, Joe, and his son, Jake. Joe, Jake, this is my daughter, Norma."

Joe offers his hand, which I shake politely. He's probably my dad's age, late forties or maybe a well-preserved fifty, but a bit broader with a slight paunch beneath his dress shirt. "The photos Lewis has shown me don't do you justice, my dear," he says complimentarily.

"Thank you." And then I turn to shake Jake's hand and freeze. Why does he look familiar? I can't place him, but something about him tickles along the periphery of my mind. He shakes my offered palm, not giving me anything to work with about how we might know each other.

We sit down to dinner, the dry chatter between Dad and Joe boring me to tears, especially as Joe waxes on about Jake joining him in the family business. But it gives me time to try to tease out the mystery of Jake.

And then like a bomb, Joe offers the answer. "Norma, I hear you're a journalism major now? Jake's in college too. Plays quarterback for the Ravens, actually." He says it with pride, patting Jake on the shoulder.

My eyes jump to Jake, who's smiling mischievously. "Yeah, I think I've seen you around campus. Seems I've heard you're *dating* one of the guys on the team, right?"

Dad chokes on his water. "You are? I didn't know that, Norma. When do I get to meet this young man?"

This cannot be happening. One, the slimeball sitting across from me is Jake Robertson, the guy who pissed Zach off so badly and almost ran him over with a fucking car in a dangerous flare of temper. Two, he just outed my relationship with Zach to my dad. No, I'm not hiding Zach in any way, and I'm actually damn proud to be with him, but there's a step-by-step to these things, and jumping from seriously-dating to meet-the-parents skips a few rather important steps.

Jake smirks, obviously pleased with himself for stirring up drama. I narrow my eyes at him, trying to figure out his game because he's got to have one. But I realize my dad is saying my name and turn to look. "When I'm ready, Dad. And not a moment before." I let the hard tone I learned from him coat the words, and he must hear the warning because he doesn't press, though the look in his eyes says this conversation is far from over.

"Yeah, I hear you've been helping Zach study quite a bit, even got his English grade up from failing to an A. A girlfriend better than any tutor. Say, you're working with him on *Paradise Lost*, right? Maybe you could read over my final essay for class too? Give me a few pointers, you know, since you're already helping him?" Every word is said with the sweetest of smiles plastered to his face, like my helping him would be the ultimate kindness. If I didn't know better, I'd even believe him. That's how well he has this good guy act down.

"Oh, I don't know about that. I'm just so busy these days. And I'm not tutoring Zach. We have study dates. I guess the extra time hitting the books is paying off for him." I let saccharin sarcasm drip from every word as I say, "I guess I'm just a good influence like that."

Jake laughs. "God knows, I need a good influence. How about we let the father figures talk business, and you meet me over at the school library? You could look at my paper really fast, and I know it'd help me so much."

Before I can say no, Dad interjects. "I'm sure Norma would love to help you, Jake."

I hiss, "Dad," and then school my features into the placid steel of my mother. "May I talk to you in the kitchen for a moment, please?" It's not a question.

He nods deferentially to Joe and follows me into the kitchen, but before I can say a word, he whispers, "Norma, I don't know what's going on out there, though I realize there's more than what's on the surface. But I also know that Joe is an old friend and a business associate I'd like to maintain a positive relationship with. So, read his paper, give him a few suggestions, and be done with it."

"Dad, I'm not some pawn to be used in your business deals, and that guy out there is basically Zach's nemesis. He's using his dad and you, and probably me. I just don't know what his end game is yet."

"Then go with him and see if you can figure it out. That's one of your special talents, isn't it? Investigate what his nefarious plan is." Though he says it like it's a silly idea, it's actually not a bad one. His voice softens, the dad I know and love and who loves me. "It's not a big deal, ladybug, unless you say no and make it one."

"Fine," I agree, though it's the last fucking thing I want to do. But Dad's right. Maybe I can use the time to figure out what Jake's up to, because he's sure as fuck up to something.

Back in the dining room, Jake is already looking smug. It doesn't help when I say, "Sure, Jake, I can go to the library now, if you want to go get your paper."

He's up out of his chair faster than a blink, gesturing for me to go first. "After you."

I give my goodbyes to Mr. Robertson and Dad, making sure to give Dad a bit of a stink eye.

AT THE LIBRARY, I SIT DOWN AT A TABLE RIGHT UP front, surrounded by people entering and exiting, grabbing snacks from the vending machine, and surrounding us at all times. I want the safety net of a crowd. I wish I could've gotten ahold of Zach on the way over, but the phone reception in the concrete-built basement weight room is non-existent.

"Okay, so . . . let me see your paper," I say brusquely as Jake comes in a minute or two after me and sits down.

Jake grins and pulls it out of his backpack. "Thank you for doing this." Something about the way he says it seems off, though he's smiling calmly.

I take it from him, careful not to touch his hand, and begin to read it over. It's fine, not great literary critique, but nothing that warrants a tutor, for damn sure. I hear my dad on one shoulder, telling me to give a few tips and suss out any ill intentions. But there's the prickly, mouthy brat Norma on my other shoulder, begging to just put it all out there and see what happens.

The devil wins.

"Your paper's fine, Jake, though I'm sure you knew that," I say, narrowing my eyes, and he has the grace to look chagrined. "So, what's this all about? Why the smokescreen? Especially when you know it's only going to cause problems with Zach and with the team."

He sits back in his chair, looking casually calm as if he hasn't a care in the world, and rubs a thumb along his bottom lip. "Look, I'm not a nice guy, or at least not always

149

a nice guy," he says with a shrug, like it's beyond his control. "But I just don't like the way Zach's treating you and I didn't know how to talk to you without the ruse. That's why I got my dad to arrange lunch with Lewis and you today. If I just came up to you randomly, I figured you'd blow me off, but I just don't think it's right and you deserve to know." He shakes his head, puppy dog eyes looking at me sadly.

I sigh, not believing his schtick for a minute but figuring that maybe this'll get me the information I'm looking for. "Fine, I'll bite. What's he saying?"

I'm expecting him to say Zach's engaging in some colorful locker room chatter. Goodness knows, he's got enough ammunition for some racy stories, though I don't think he'd blab like that. What I'm not expecting are Jake's next words.

"He keeps talking about how he needed a tutor and Coach set him up with some fake girlfriend thing to cover it up, but that he's such a fucking god that he turned it into a pussy-on-demand situation for the semester. Basically, he says he just uses you as a place to stick his dick, if you'll pardon the vulgarity." His tone is sincere and disgusted, like he can't believe someone would say that.

There's so much information in what he just said that I can't even process it all at once, and instead, I have to take it in bits and chunks. My mind whirls.

Okay, there is no way, I mean literally no way, Zach is talking about me like I'm a cum receptacle with no emotions, not after everything we've shared. And the mere fact that I don't even consider that a possibility speaks volumes about just how far we've come. No doubt, no second thoughts, no insecurity. I know without question that Jake is lying about that and using the obscene insult to poke at my emotions, expecting my horror.

But I'm not horrified. I'm furious but force the explosion of words bubbling in my throat down as I consider the rest of what Jake said.

Tutor. Fake girlfriend. That was our original cover story. But no one is supposed to know that. Just me and Zach. Coach and Erica. And it's certainly not true now. I don't think it ever really was.

I wonder if Jake overhead Coach talking about it to Zach or maybe to someone else? He is around the locker room with the rest of the guys, so it's definitely possible, I suppose.

And then an image pops in my head. Of Erica in full Ravens gear. Like a super fan. Like a . . . groupie.

And though I have no reason to think Jake and Erica know each other, every instinct I have says that's who told him the whole secret setup.

Jake looks at me expectantly, waiting with a sad face for my breakdown, but I can see the eager glee in his eyes. I take the fastest second to compose my thoughts and then strike.

"Tell me, is Erica part of your whole evil plot to destroy Zach? Or did she just share some pillow talk after what

I'm sure was a disappointing fuck?" My face is stoic, nothing more than mere curiosity.

Jake's jaw drops. "What? Erica didn't say shit, and she's a better fuck than you are. I know because Zach's been mouthing."

I smirk. "Oh, so you *do* know Erica? The editor of *The Chronicle*, who it seems is rather unable to keep her mouth shut. Kind of an important skill for a reporter, wouldn't you say?" Anger lights up in his eyes, and though I know it's a dangerous button to push, I can't stop my mouth. "And I wasn't talking about her being a shitty fuck. I was talking about you, *Snake*." I say it like it's beyond obvious that it's the most ironic nickname in the world, like the guys in the locker room who called him that were joking about his size, or the lack thereof.

"You fucking bitch! I was this-fucking-close to finally getting my shot. Zach was almost failing, mostly on his own right, but a little cash here or there never hurt, and it was going to be mine. I should be the star quarterback of the Ravens, the one the team looks up to, the one the scouts come to watch, the one headed for the pros. And if it wasn't for that fucking contract-blocker, it would be me. Me!"

His anger is getting out of control, his voice louder, and we're drawing an audience in the quiet of the library. I'm pretty sure I even see a few cell phones recording Jake's apparent breakdown, and he follows my glance around, seeing the attention centered on him. But though he seems to want it on the field, deserved or not, right now, he wants out of the limelight.

He grabs his paper and backpack, slinging it over one shoulder as he points at me, saying loudly enough for everyone to hear, "Fucking whore . . . sold your pussy to the quarterback. And for what? An interview with Coach? You're worse than a whore. You're a cheap slut."

There's a collective gasp, and then Jake stomps out of the library. All eyes turn to me, questions and judgments and concern in every one of them. I dig for a shield, throwing up some sass, and say with a tiny laugh, "Sold my pussy to the quarterback? He means my *boyfriend*. And trust me, I gave it freely because . . . have you seen him? Whoo!" I let a saucy smile take my face, and my weird response seems to have put most folks off. I guess they were waiting for my breakdown too. Fucking vultures.

I grab my bag, knowing that Zach's in the weight room and that I need to talk to him now. And Coach. And Erica.

But Zach first.

CHAPTER 15

"*A*ll right, man. Throw that weight up and give me three. I got you covered," Tim Perkins, one of the wide receivers, tells me. I spread my hands wide on the cool metal bar, pressing it up before lowering the weight to my chest. I do the three reps and set it back on the rack.

Standing up, I stretch a bit. "Okay, your turn," I say as we switch places and he lies down on the bench.

All around us are guys working out. It's not the whole team because it's not an official practice or mandatory weight session, but it's understood that unless you have class or class-related shit, you'd better have your ass in here pumping some iron.

Music is blaring, the guys are bro-ing out as we smack talk about the upcoming game, and it's like I'm home. These guys are my family and I'll be sad to see them go when the season's over. Not everyone is leaving, of course, and there is plenty of off-season work to do, but some of the guys are graduating, and others get side-tracked with different priorities when there's not a game every week.

The warm, fuzzy moment comes to a screeching halt when the door swings open and Norma walks in. No, that's not right. She doesn't walk in. She blows in like a fucking hurricane, fire in her eyes, and I swear her red hair is blowing in some sort of invisible wind because she's crackling with fury.

I can't help it. My first instinct is to think . . . *what did I do*? But then I see beneath the whirling storm to my Norma. And she's scared shitless.

"Brat! What's wrong?" I yell. Someone chooses that moment to turn the music off and my voice echoes in the sudden silence.

"We need to talk. Now." Every man knows that those are words you don't want to hear, and the guys around me cringe. Norma must see their reactions because she restates, "Not like that. But we need to talk. Where's Coach Jefferson?"

I'm thoroughly confused now. Why does Norma want to talk to Coach? "Uhm, his office, probably. But . . . why?"

She doesn't answer, just gives me one of those looks that silently communicates a thousand words. And I realize that this is about us and the tutoring. That's the only reason she'd need to see Coach. "C'mon."

I grab her hand and drag her down the hall, knocking hard twice but opening the door at the same time. "Coach . . . sorry to interrupt, but—"

Norma doesn't give me a chance to play nice. "Coach Jefferson, I'm Norma Blackstone, Zach's girlfriend and *tutor*." Her emphasis on the word is intentional, giving it a deeper meaning that Coach instantly catches.

"Yeah, yeah. Come in, I guess? What can I do for you?" Coach asks.

Norma sits down in the chair in front of the desk uninvited but stays perched on the edge, leaning forward. Coach sits down too, hands crossed in front of him.

"Sir, this is a lot. Please, let me see if I can get this all out." She takes a big breath, as if she's about to spill the longest story ever and needs oxygen to do so. "I work for Erica Waters at *The Chronicle*. I'm the one she asked to do that favor for you and tutor Zach with the whole fake girlfriend thing."

Coach gets up, holding a staying hand out, and Norma pauses as he shuts the door. When he sits back down, she continues. "Today, Jake Robertson schemed to get me alone at the library—"

"What the fuck?" I yell.

Norma grabs my hand, holding it tightly. "My dad asked me to do it as a favor. He didn't know," she tells me before she looks back to Coach. "I didn't know just how unhinged Jake has become." She lets that sink in for a moment. "He said he needed help with a paper, but it was a ploy. He tried to tell me that Zach was saying uhm, *unflattering things* about me, about us."

I interrupt again. I can't help it. "What did that asshole say now?"

Norma blushes but she says it without a tremble. "He said that you were using me for sex, basically that we're still fake but that I'm the only one who doesn't realize that."

"Mother fucker, I'm gonna kill him." I turn to the door but stop when Coach growls.

"Son, you'd best sit your ass down in that chair and shut your mouth. Let the woman speak, for fuck's sake." He gives me a hard look, but even years of training to listen to my coach's instructions without question aren't enough to hold me back from tracking Jake down right this fucking minute. But what is? Norma looks at me, eyes pleading for me to do as Coach says, so begrudgingly, I do. But only until she's done, then I'm Snake hunting.

Norma looks at me. "Obviously, I didn't believe him." Her words shoot to my heart. I hadn't considered for a moment that she would believe something so ridiculous, but then I remember how unsure my Brat used to be. But when someone basically told her that her worst nightmare was true, she didn't doubt. Didn't doubt me, or herself, or us. It's a beautiful ray of sunshine in the midst of this shit.

"But more importantly, I realized that he said Zach was mouthing about his *tutor* and his *fake girlfriend*." She emphasizes the words but doesn't give me time to process what that means before continuing, "No one knew, at least no one was supposed to. I did a bit of quick deduction and realized that football groupie Erica told him. And though he didn't exactly mean to, Jake confirmed it. He got really angry then, stood up and started yelling about how Zach was almost failing on his own but that 'a little cash never hurt', implying that he bribed Zach's English teacher, I'm guessing to grade him poorly and cost him his eligibility, so that Jake could play. He went on a bit of a rant, and the theme was basically me, me, me."

Coach huffs. "Shit. That's . . . a lot." He shakes his head a bit and then seems to pull it together, but there's a knock at the door. "Not now, go the fuck away."

But the door opens anyway and Will pops his head through the crack. "Sorry to interrupt, but sir, you need to see this." He holds up his phone and Coach holds his hand out to take it. He clicks the *Play* button in the middle of the screen and Jake's voice fills the room. It seems one of those people who were filming his tirade posted it online.

Coach watches it through twice and then hands the phone back to Will, who's looking at me with unspoken promises in his eyes. "Send me that, please. If you'll excuse me, I have some business to take care of."

Norma and I stand, hearing the dismissal. "Of course, sir. Me too."

"Stop right there, Zach." I turn to look at him, and he steps right up to me, invading my space. He's a big man, but several inches shorter than me. Even still, I have no doubt he could make me cry uncle. "Let me be clear. I want you to stay here while I get this shit sorted out. You are not, in any circumstances, to approach, speak to, or lay a hand on Jake Robertson. The last thing I need is his daddy getting you arrested for being a dumbass. Do I make myself clear?"

"Sir—" I try to argue.

But he cuts me off, turning to Will. "Senior Captain, I think I need you to take the defensive line, and anyone else who wants to go, out for some drills on the field tonight. Really make sure everyone's working together as a team. But I need every one of you, all of my star players, ready for the game this weekend. Understood?" Will nods his head and then looks at me.

Coach just gave them the go-ahead to go after Jake. Without me. I hate that they're fighting my battle for me once again, especially when this one is so damn personal, but I know I'd do the same thing for them. And as mad as I am, I don't know that I'd stop at beating the shit out of Jake. And Coach is right. I can't be stupid about this or Jake wins and I lose anyway.

Coach walks us back down the hall, already on his phone. "Yes, Dean, I need to have an emergency meeting with us, Erica Waters, Jake Robertson, and Professor Ledbetter. Yes, right now."

Back in the weight room, the guys are all looking at their phones, so I know they've seen the video of Jake. Will gathers everyone up and says, "Drill time." Usually, there'd be a few moans of whining about having to hit the field, but tonight, everyone knows it's something different and there's a chorus of 'Fucking right, it's drill time.' and 'Hell, yeah.' As the guys file out, they each give me a high-five or touch their forehead to mine, assuring me that the team has my back and that we protect our own, even when it's from an internal threat.

Lenny is the last to walk out, and after fist-bumping me, he stops in front of Norma. "Don't you worry. We all know you aren't a whore. You're a goddamn magician who got my boy here locked down. And Norma, you've got some big clanging brass balls on you. Badass bitch." Norma beams at the praise.

And then we're alone.

I'm so on edge I think I'm going to crawl out of my damn skin. I'm pacing, hot anger pumping through my veins, encouraging me to scour the campus and find Jake. Or at a minimum, to follow Coach and demand some answers. But Norma stops me with a soft touch.

"Hey, calm down. It's going to be okay, Zach. Coach is handling Erica and Professor Ledbetter, though is it wrong of me to hope Jake misses that meeting because he's running drills with the team?" She does little air quotes so I know she caught on to what's happening tonight. I have a split second of question on whether she's down for back-alley justice, but then she spits out, "I hope they find that fucker before I do because he'll get off easier with them than with me."

I smirk at her trash-talking. "You are so sexy when you're being all bitchy and bratty. Like fire personified, inside and out. My little fire fairy brat."

My answer seems to surprise her, shocking her out of her flash of anger too. "Oh, that wasn't bratty. That was a reality check." A tiny smile tilts her lips. "Okay, maybe a bit bratty."

Needing to touch her, I pull her to me, crushing her in my arms. "Fuck, Norma. This is so messed up. I never thought he'd—"

She cuts me off with a kiss, and I realize that we don't need words right now. We need each other.

Though he didn't stand a chance at driving a wedge between the two of us, Jake's threat is dangerous in a different way. The thought reminds me of how pleased I am that Norma didn't question us for a second, that not only have we come so far, but she has come so far. Still my mouthy Brat who takes no shit but dishes out prickly barbs with laser accuracy, but also my girl who knows that she's mine and I'm hers, unequivocally.

Our kisses become more frantic. "Norma, I need you."

"I need you too. Take me," she says, panting for air.

I reach up, encircling her neck with my hands for a moment, and she freezes, mouth open and eyes wide, saying yes without words. I untie the silk scarf there and then pick her up, carrying her across the room.

"What is this thing?" she asks, looking at the big metal rack above her.

"You'll love this. It's a power rack," I say, chuckling. I pull her shirt and bra off unceremoniously but lay a quick kiss to her sternum as she shudders. She offers her hands, and I tie the scarf around one wrist. "Hands up, Brat, and look in the mirror."

The air, or maybe it's the anticipation, raises goose-bumps along her arms as I loop the scarf over the pullup bar and tie her other wrist. Like usual, it's not tight, but it's become our thing and she so willingly and beautifully gives herself to me each and every time this way, wanting it as much as I do.

The automatic lights have cycled off, leaving portions of the room in shadow and little pockets of light from the spotlights in the ceiling. Right above Norma, a beam shines down, highlighting her body in sharp relief, shadows and light dancing along her skin. "You look fucking glorious, Norma." In response to my words, her nipples harden, tempting me to lick, suck, and bite.

I pull her skirt down, tossing it aside after she steps out of it, and grab her ass, massaging her cheeks in my big hands. She whimpers, pressing back for more, so I wrap my arms around her and grind my cock against her ass. Even through my workout shorts, my cock tries to penetrate her.

But I need to taste her first. I drop to my knees, kissing along her spine and then biting her sweet ass. She steps wide without my telling her, and I use my hands to guide her to arch her back, letting me see all of her. I lean in, and she moans needily, so I spread her cheeks and tease at her puckered hole.

She lets out a keening cry. "Oh, God, Zach." I do it again, and then go lower, tasting her honey and circling her clit. Her hips sway, and I focus on her clit, letting a finger slip inside her tight pussy. She covers me in cream, and I spread it up to her ass, tapping on her rosebud as I lick her clit. Her cries become incoherent, just high-pitched sounds, begging, and then she shatters.

Her body shudders and I lap at her juices, wanting to

swallow every drop. Needing to be inside her, I stand up, shoving my workout shorts down at the same time.

The head of my cock slips inside her, and we both groan. "Everything's going to be okay, Brat. You're all mine," I whisper as I fill her up.

"I am," she confirms. I'm still for a moment, letting her adjust, and I think I hear something. A thud, maybe? But it sounds far away.

I meet her eyes in the silvery mirror where she's watching like I told her to. "You'll have to be quiet so we don't get caught fucking in the weight room. Pretty sure that's against the team's rules." Her pussy clenches around me, and I know she likes the thought of being naughty.

I start stroking in and out of her, and I know she wants to push back against me, but the scarf is holding her, forcing her to stand tall. I like her at my mercy, but I can't tease her right now, both of us needing to connect on a physical level and deeper.

I speed up until we're both trembling, gasping. "Is this what you want, Brat?"

"Fuck . . . yes!" Suddenly, I hear a sound again and freeze, not pulling out but keeping her full of cock. I barely move, just grind my cock back and forth slowly against that rough spot deep inside her, careful not to push her over so we don't make a sound.

When I don't hear anything for a few seconds, I give her one powerful thrust. Her air rushes out. "Zach!"

"That's it, Norma. I'm gonna fuck you and fill you with

all I've got, reward you for knowing that you belong to me. And I sure as fuck belong to you." My words are whispered, growls that vibrate against the silky skin of her back.

My hips slap against her ass as I fuck her deeply, our breath coming in short gasps as we both get closer and closer. Her pussy squeezes around my thick cock like a vice, and I clamp my teeth down to hold back the roar as I explode, my cock coming deep inside her.

She's watching in the mirror as I come, and it triggers her orgasm too. She whimpers, biting her lip, but she's still louder than she probably should be. It makes me feel like a beast that I can make her forget herself that way.

When we catch our breaths, I reach up and untie her wrists, massaging her fingers. "Why do you do it?" I ask as I kiss each fingertip. "You don't have to let me tie you up. It doesn't really matter to me. I've never done that with anyone but you."

"I know I don't have to," she says softly, laying a sweet kiss to the corner of my mouth. "But, Zach, sometimes, I feel like there's all this pressure on my shoulders to do amazing things and be this hard-hitting powerhouse. But you help me understand that by surrendering to you, by letting you be in charge, you make me stronger. I feel like can breathe and just . . . *be*."

I smile and kiss her squarely on the lips. "With you by my side, I'm stronger too. And better, like I have a purpose beyond the field."

We pull our clothes back on as we talk quietly, making

sure the room is reset so no one is the wiser, and heading down the dim hallway. I don't know where we're going, but I can't stay here any longer. If nothing else, we'll go to Norma's place until I get word from Coach or Will that things are handled.

"I don't know anyone stronger," she says with a smirk. "You're going to make one hell of a pro quarterback."

I nod, her confidence in me a boost but nothing compared to the thought deep in my heart. "And if everything goes the way I dream, I'll be playing in big games and signing big contracts."

She thinks that's all I had to say and smiles before adding, "Big records too."

"Fifty," I say with a smile. "I think that's a good start."

She looks at me, confusion in her eyes. "Fifty?" As we step out of the building, the late November chill surrounds us. I pause to pull my jacket off and lay it around Norma's shoulders. She slips her arms into the sleeves, but she's basically drowning in it, the cuffs hanging well past her hands.

"Fifty years. Of marriage. That's the main record I want, just like my parents. They're not there yet, but they will be. That's what I want. More than football, though I seriously want that too. But I want someone to share it all with, to be in the stands cheering me on, to make a life with during football and after football."

She looks up at me. "That sounds . . . nice. Are you thinking about anyone in particular?" She's grinning, but there's more hope than tease in her voice.

I chuckle, pulling her close. "Brat, I think you and I are thinking the same damn thing."

She lifts to her tiptoes, and I bend down to catch her lips in a kiss, but just before I make contact, a loud voice calls out, "Payback, bitch!"

I try to push Norma behind me, not sure of the threat but wanting to protect her regardless, but she twists in my arms and then cries out in pain as there's a loud crash.

She's panting as a dark figure pushes past me. Before I can think, I lower her to the floor, and though she's crying from the pain, she's chanting, "I'm okay, I'm okay." I take her at her word, and with a quick kiss to her forehead, I take off after the shadowy attacker.

CHAPTER 16

"*9*-1-1, what's your emergency?"

I yell as I run, making fast headway at catching up with the ghost who's zigging and zagging as he runs. "Ravens football complex, a guy just jumped me and my girlfriend. She's been hit in the leg."

I have a good idea who's in front of me, and red rage seeps into my vision as I pour on the speed to chase him down. Talking with the phone in my hand is slowing me down, though. "Sir?"

"My girlfriend was attacked," I repeat, forcing my voice to be as calm as possible. "Parking lot, the Ravens football practice complex. Send campus cops and a fucking ambulance. I'm chasing the motherfucker who did this."

"Sir, that's not a good idea—"

I hang up my phone, dropping it to the pavement as I sprint harder. I use both arms and force my breathing into a rhythm as I close the gap quickly, tackling him from behind.

"You motherfucker," I growl as we roll on the ground. He gets a punch in to my face, but I quickly pin him down, ripping off his mask. I'm not surprised. "I fucking knew it."

"I–I didn't mean to hit her," Jake stammers, holding his hands up. "I was going after you!"

"You mistook a five-foot-four girl for me because of what? A team jacket?" I ask, my voice dripping with fury as I yank his shoulders up with a fistful of his shirt. Before Jake can respond, I punch him in the nose, enjoying the satisfying crunch of his bone under my blow.

Jake tries to fight back, but my rage has inoculated me to pain. Instead, I hammer him again and again, smashing his face with all my might.

"I'm sorry!" Jake howls, his eyes already getting puffy from the blows.

"Not as sorry as you're going to be," I rasp, every instance of him undermining me on the field, trying to get me hurt with wrong signals, almost running me over with his car, and most of all, hurting Norma, riding me hard and giving me an ugly desire to destroy him.

I'm staring down at him in disgust when suddenly I hear a scream. "Zach!"

It's Norma, and her obvious cry of pain pierces through the hot fire of my anger. I scramble from the ground, needing to get to her, but I yell back, "Don't you fucking move. The cops are the way."

He tries to crawl, belly dragging the dirty ground, but I know he won't get far.

I crouch next to Norma, brushing the hair back from her forehead. Her eyes meet mine, utter agony and incomprehension mixing in equal measure. "Fuck, Zach. It hurts so bad. Why?"

"It was Jake," I tell her, putting a hand on her shoulder to keep her still. She keeps trying to sit up, but I can tell by the way her leg is lying, she shouldn't be moving. "He meant to hit me."

"Why?" Norma repeats, her own pain making her not understand. Instead of trying to explain any more, I hold her, letting her pour her agony against my chest.

"I'm so sorry, Norma. The ambulance should be here soon," I tell her as the sound of the siren gets louder.

Norma sobs, her tears soaking my shirt before the ambulance and cops arrive. Unsure what the hell's going on, they let me ride with her to the hospital, although I do notice that a cop car follows us as well.

The whole time, I apologize to Norma, who's crying and whimpering with every bump in the road. She whispers through her pain. "How bad is it?"

I glance over at the paramedic, who seems unsure. "I don't think it's that bad, but we don't know for sure. I think it's a clean break, but they'll get X-rays and everything at the hospital."

"Even if it's broken, don't worry," I tell her, putting on my best face. "We'll rehab together, Brat, and you'll be kicking ass in powder puff before next season."

That at least gets Norma to sniffle and smile a little, though it's more of a grimace. "There is no powder puff football at our school."

I give her hand a little squeeze, trying to force a smile at her. "Then I'll start a league, and you can be the star player."

When we get to the hospital, Norma has to roll into an exam room to get checked out and the nurses stop me at the door, saying that they need room to work and will come get me soon.

That's when the cops start by getting me into a conference room. I try to answer their questions as honestly as I can, but my brain's running a hundred miles an hour while at the same time, it seems to be going in slow motion.

"So you hit the girl, then—" the one cop, a detective with a permanent 'fuck you' scowl on his face, starts.

I shake my head, trying by sheer will alone to not jump out of the chair and yell at him. "No. Jake hit Norma, and I chased him down. Norma's my girlfriend. Why would I hurt her?"

"Well, why would this Jake fellow hit her?" he asks. "Is this some love triangle gone wrong?"

Before I can argue, there's a big commotion and a man in a custom-tailored suit comes in. Behind him is a cute girl I've seen Norma with in pictures. So if this is

Arianna, then he must be . . . "I'm Liam Blackstone. Zach Knight?"

I nod, and the cop looks like he's about to pop a gasket. "Mr. Blackstone, I'm sorry, but—"

"Zach is done talking," Liam says, handing the cop a card. "Here's my attorney's card. Mr. Knight has nothing to say until he gets here."

The cop grumbles, then nods. "Fine. Mr. Knight, you're not under arrest, but don't leave the hospital just yet."

He leaves, and in the muted hospital silence, Liam and I study each other.

He tilts his head, appraising me, and I'm not sure if he's going to find me lacking, especially considering tonight's happenings. He must find me acceptable somehow, though, because he continues, "Who hurt my sister?"

"Jake Robertson. He's my backup quarterback on the team and has been gunning for me all season. He tried to involve Norma today, but we didn't dream he'd do something like . . . this." My voice breaks, and I plop back to the chair, my head buried in my hands.

"Robertson . . . I know that name," Liam growls after a moment, his fists bunching. Liam might be about fifty pounds lighter than me, but he looks like he could handle himself well. He's certainly built well enough. "Where is he?"

"Probably getting treatment too. I nearly curbstomped him after I chased him down and caught him," I admit. "Might have charges coming my way because of it, actually."

Liam shakes his head, pulling out his phone. "Not when my lawyers are done. Arianna, could you go out to the lobby and get with the doctors and see if you can get an update? I'll talk with the campus cops. I want every security camera in the vicinity of the football complex pulled and one of our lawyers with the cops when they go over it. Tonight. Oh . . . and Zach should probably call Coach Jefferson. I figure he'll want to know as well."

Arianna nods before stepping out. Liam dials a number, and his conversation is brief. "Dad? It's Liam. Norma was attacked at school by Jake Robertson. Yes, *that* Robertson. Figured you should know. I'm at the hospital. I'll give you an update as soon as I hear something, but get here when you can. 'Bye."

Liam hangs up and then looks at me. "So . . . rumor has it you've been seeing my sister."

I stand up, offering him a hand since this is crazily our first time to meet, though I feel like I know him from Norma's stories about her big brother who always made time for her. "I'm more than seeing her, but yes."

He shakes my hand, squeezing harder than need be, and I squeeze back. We have a bit of a staring contest and then he asks, "How much more?"

I let go of his hand and give him a nod. "I think I'll discuss that with her first. But she's the most important thing in my life."

"Even more important than football? You're supposed to have a pretty bright future on the field," he says doubtfully.

I nod, clearing my throat. "Even more than football, and I don't say that lightly."

He smiles. "All right then. Let's see what my brat of a sister is up to." I flinch and he notices. "What?"

I know my face must be turning pink because I can feel the heat. "Uhm, that's what I call her. Brat." His eyes narrow, and I rush to explain, "But it's a . . . term of endearment."

He pales, then chuckles. "And I will never call her that again. All you, man."

It's awkward as fuck but also feels like some spark of male connection was just forged between us. I don't think we're ever going to play Never Have I Ever or some shit, but I think we could probably grab a beer sometime. After this mess is done.

About fifteen minutes later, the doctors come and get the two of us. Norma's still in an exam room, her left leg in a Velcro splint, but she's smiling as the curtain opens. "Hey . . . Arianna told me you two talked. That must've been *awkward*." Her voice lilts at the end.

"Hey, Little Sis," Liam says, taking her left hand. "They have you on the good stuff?"

"I'm flying high," Norma agrees. She squeezes Liam's hand, then looks at me. "Zach . . . ohmygawd, I'm so sorry."

I shake my head, tears threatening at the corners of my eyes. "You've got nothing to be sorry for. I should be apologizing to you, Norma. This whole fucking thing is my fault. Jake was after me."

Norma forces her tossing head to still, eyes meeting mine, and for a second, I think she's lucid. But then she singsongs, "Fuck, you're so pretty. I love you so much. Did you know that? I love you, Zach."

I can't help the grin that splits my face, and Liam shrugs. I chuckle, bending down to tell her, "I love you too, Brat."

"Ooh, yeah . . . I'm your Brat. Hey, do you think when they let me outta here, you could tie my hands behind my back again? Or—oh—maybe over the hood of the car again? Yeah, that!"

Liam clears his throat, his cheeks blushing now. "I, uh, think I'll step out for a minute. Check on Arianna's progress on her to-do list."

I lift one shoulder, some version of an attempt at 'sorry, man' for his having to hear that. Something tells me that while Norma won't remember this conversation at all, Liam and I are never going to forget it. Though he's probably going to remember being mortified at his little sister's sex life, I'm going to remember it as the first time we said *I love you*.

CHAPTER 17

*A*few days later, after a quick surgery to reset the bones in my leg, I'm finally home, albeit with a clunky cast that reaches from my toes to just below my knee.

"You're actually tough as steel now, Sis," Liam tells me teasingly.

"The metal they used is actually . . . ti-tan-iuumm," I sing loudly and badly. Liam busts out laughing and I grin back.

"When's your next appointment? Do you need me to take you?" He already has his calendar app open on his phone like he's going to add my appointment to his to-do list. But I know he's already got the appointment listed there because he's Liam.

"No, Zach said he'd take me. Doc said I'd need a check this week to make sure nothing's changed since I was discharged from the hospital and then another follow-up in four weeks, and then hopefully, the last one two to four weeks after that when I get my cast off. Then, the fun of physical therapy starts." I shudder a bit at the memory of my orthopedic surgeon telling me that the real work of healing started on my first day of PT and that it was going to be hard and painful, but absolutely necessary. "Zach already said he'll work with me on that too. I think he's got some vision of us being workout buddies. Like he's going to cheer me on for every rep of toe point and flex, and then I'm gonna fall into his arms, grateful for his time and patience. I'm expecting it's going to end up with me whiny and bitchy about how hard it is and him smacking me and telling me to 'suck it up, buttercup' in some growly amalgamation of every football coach he's ever had."

Liam opens his mouth and then promptly clacks it shut, his eyebrows going high.

"What?" I ask, curious of what just ran through his mind.

He shakes his head. "I was going to make a joke about you liking it when he smacks you, but then I remembered your drug-induced tell-all and decided I didn't really want to know any more details than you've already over-shared."

I blush, mortified at the things I apparently was spouting off, loudly and vehemently, when I was medicated. Liam hasn't teased me too badly, but Zach has given me so much shit for it that I threatened to never let him tie me up again. But when he'd mimicked my high voice, 'I looove it when you tie me up, Zach . . . can you do it again?' I'd eventually laughed and given in because I was telling the truth and I do love it. No need to punish myself for my mouthiness, not when Zach can do that for me.

"Yeah, maybe it's best that we skip those jokes. I'm friends with Arianna now, too, you know? I might know a little more about my brother than I'd like to."

We meet eyes, silently agreeing to never speak of this again. "So, the game starting?"

"Yes, the game. Let's watch the game," I say. Liam hits the kitchen for a few drinks, a bottle of beer for him and a Coke for me since I can't mix anything stronger with my medications.

Sitting on the couch, just the two of us, reminds me of our younger days when a teenage Liam would voluntarily give up his Saturday mornings to watch cartoons with a younger me. It's not the usual cartoons and movie marathons we once had, but watching my man play the game he loves with Liam by my side is a nice progression.

When the Ravens win the conference championship, we're both yelling so loudly that my neighbor downstairs bangs on the ceiling. We try to quiet down our celebration, especially since I know the poor lady is going to have to deal with me stomping around clad in a cast for the next two months. No need to start off on the wrong foot now. I grin to myself at the stupid joke . . . the wrong foot.

Hours later, I almost have to pinch myself at the vision in front of me. Actually, that's not a bad idea considering these pain meds pack a wallop of a punch. Maybe

I am hallucinating. "Ouch!" I say. "Nope, not a dream, I guess."

Zach reaches for my hand, stopping me from pinching myself again just to be sure. "Why the hell are you pinching yourself, Brat?" Liam clears his throat, and Zach rephrases, "You okay, *Norma*?" He gives Liam a mildly apologetic look, but I can tell he's not the least bit sorry. It's just what he calls me and I like being his brat. God knows, everyone at this table knows what a pill I can be.

I look around the table at the people surrounding me, the ones who put up with my shit willingly and lovingly. Zach's question means every eye is on me, and I meet each one with a smile. Zach, Liam, Adrianna, Dad, and Mom. "Just so glad you're all here. It means a lot," I say, choking up. Tears threaten at the corners of my eyes.

Liam groans. "Fuck, you broke her, dude. She never used to cry before you. She'd just smack talk us all about not having anything better to do on a Saturday night than crowding around her tiny ass table."

His outburst makes everyone laugh a bit, breaking the spell and giving me a moment to compose myself. I grin through the drying tears. "I'd like to think maybe he fixed me more than broke me, but if you'd rather me go back to busting your balls, that can be arranged. In fact, Arianna was just telling me the other day—"

"No," he interrupts, and Arianna laughs, shaking her head and clearly mouthing, 'I told her nothing.'

Dad's voice is a bit louder than need be, but it does the trick, getting everyone to quiet down about things that would probably make Mom's socialite crowd faint. "So, Zach, tell me about the game, the team. It seems the drama didn't interfere with the win."

Zach straightens, unconsciously sitting taller. He's relatively comfortable with my dad after they both spent the last few days sitting by my hospital bedside, but I think there's always that little spark of fear when a guy talks to his girl's dad. "The team was a bit shook up, understandably, but we pulled together and did our best. Coach Buckley had my back on offense, and Coach Jefferson kept the whole team solid. We're proud, not just of the win today, but of the way we played as a whole."

Dad grins. "Damn fine interview answer. Guess my daughter's been coaching you on what to say to reporters too?" He looks to me proudly.

But Zach corrects him. "No sir, Norma's a damn smart girl and has definitely helped me out with school and so much more, but I've been talking to the press for years. I know what to say, and if I didn't, Coach Jefferson would've held me back from ever seeing a microphone."

My dad smiles at the bold answer.

"Hey, speaking of school . . . what did Coach say about his meeting with the dean? Everything got a bit crazy and I never heard, or if someone told me, the conversation washed away with the pain meds," I ask Zach.

Zach grimaces. "It was bad, honestly. Professor Ledbetter lost her job since she wasn't tenured, and taking bribes to change a student's grades is a pretty serious offense. She admitted she did that early in the semester but got cold feet, and my later work was more correctly scored, but she did change all of my papers and quizzes to their appropriate grade. At least she still had copies to do that with. I easily have a B-plus, might even that A I've been wanting if I ace the final essay."

"I'll help with that! Not like I'm doing much else, sitting here for the next few days. Oh, and thanks for getting my paperwork from my professors, Arianna. Most of it can all be done online. My math professor even offered to let my study group leader film the lecture so I could watch it at home. But there's always those few things that need to be handed in or returned old-school-style on paper. I should be able to stay pretty caught up, though, and not affect my grades too much."

Arianna smiles. "Happy to help. Don't you have an article to write too, though? That's going to be a big chunk of work, so don't overdo it." Her motherly words are sweet, and judging by the look on my mom's face, she approved of this message of over-restraint. She probably asked Arianna to say it since I'd begged her to chill after the fiftieth time she'd tried to force me back on the couch. A mother's love. Can't live without it . . . can't live with it, sometimes, I think faux-sourly. Truth is, my mom has been a pillar of support, and there were some moments before surgery that I really just wanted my mommy and she was right there by my bedside, soothing my fears away like moms do.

"I do need to work on the write-up. Trey, he's the newly-promoted editor, stopped by while I was in the hospital to see if I wanted to write it or have someone else do it. I demanded the assignment, of course," I say, throwing my hands out to the side as if there'd been any chance I would turn that opportunity down.

Trey seems like a nice guy, but when he'd come by to introduce himself as my new boss, I'd been surprised. Apparently, Erica resigned as editor, though legally, she didn't do anything wrong. She wasn't involved in Jake's plans, but her sex-induced loose lips were a catalyst, and she'd burned some bridges with the administration, our paper staff, the whole football team, and Coach Jefferson. I think she mostly wants to just finish out her senior year with as little attention as possible, but she did send me a text that simply said, *I'm so sorry*.

Trey told me that my position with the paper was secure, but not to think that my in with the football team would get me any more bylines than any other lowly reporter learning the ropes. I'd smiled and told him I didn't want any special favors and most definitely don't want to be the sports column reporter, but that I'd be happy to write a few football team-centric pieces from interviews with the guys and coach about the incident, sprinkling in my own injury at the end.

He'd agreed and told me to 'be careful with those crazy football guys.' He'd had a teasing smirk, and I could appreciate the humor with Zach at my side and in light of Jake's actions, though I refused to shrink away like some broken victim.

"Make sure you include the final penalties for Jake Robertson too. It should be more, so much more, but I did the best I could for you, ladybug. I'm so sorry I ever pushed you to help him." His words are broken, his guilt at having had any hand in this obvious.

"Dad, you didn't do anything wrong. I was pissed at the time, and no, I don't want to be involved in your business dealings." I quickly correct myself, "Unless you're setting me up for an interview, of course. But none of us had any idea that Jake was going to go off the rails like that. I'm not sure he even knew the pressure was getting to him and it was that dire of a situation."

In the end, Jake's injuries had been significantly worse than mine. He'd had a broken nose and cheekbone from Zach's punches, and when he fell, he'd hit the pavement wrong and had some internal bleeding. He'd been placed under arrest while still in his hospital bed, hand-cuffed to the railing as the police read him his rights and stationed a guard outside his door.

His dad, Joe, had raged about his son being treated like a common criminal and had hired some big-shot lawyer to launch his defense.

That was when Dad had taken over and the whole thing had turned into a twisted version of a business negotiation. I forget sometimes what a cold, calculating monster my Dad can be when the situation calls for it, and hurting his only daughter had triggered some pretty serious viciousness for him. But through it all, he was the dad I've always known, powerful and strong but soft and sweet to me.

I think dealing with all of that might've even brought Dad and Liam together a bit, allies against a shared foe. They're never going to be tight, but at least they're both here together, something that was previously a rare occurrence.

In the end, Jake plead guilty to assault for his attack on me, and attempted manslaughter for almost running Zach over, because you can be sure that Liam got the parking lot video for that too. We each got a permanent restraining order against him too. Jake won't do time, but he's on a parole for a long time and has to do anger management classes and seek help for some daddy issues that were worse than we'd ever thought. He was expelled from school too, so no more football.

I won't say I feel sorry for him, because I don't, but I can imagine that having your whole life implode, especially when it's through your own doing, is hard. I just hope he gets better and stays the fuck away from Zach and me.

After dinner, everyone is slow to leave. Mom, especially, offers to tuck me in or set up a work station in the living room, but I reassure her that I'm fine and that Zach will be here to help. That seems to make her smile, and I guess she approves of Zach wholeheartedly, because she leaves without my Dad having to drag her out like he has the last few times.

I lie back on the couch, my head on the arm and my foot propped up high on the couch back. "Ahh, alone at last," I say, a smile on my face though my eyes are already closing.

"You tired, Brat?" Zach asks, and though it's a sweet question, like he's ready to tuck me in if I say yes, I can hear something more in the undercurrent.

I crack one eye. "Maybe. Why?"

He smirks. "Oh, if you're tired, I'll let you rest. I just

thought with me winning the championship today, you might want to celebrate a bit."

My other eye opens, all thoughts of sleep evaporating at his cocky look. The one that's pointedly looking me over, head to toe. Sexy as fuck . . . well, until he hits my cast. "Actually, maybe I should let you rest. You've had a long day."

"Scared of a cast, Zach? I promise not to bang you over the head with it if you bang me." It's a stupid joke, not even funny, but it makes Zach laugh and reconsider.

"You sure you're okay, Brat?" he asks, and I know if I said no, he'd patiently take care of me all night.

"I'm okay, except that I need you inside me. It's been days, Zach. And after everything, I just . . . I need you." My voice is soft, no filter and no façade, just raw truth.

Zach lies down on top of me, his thickening cock pressed right up against my pussy as he holds himself up. He watches my face to make sure he's not hurting me, but my leg is supported and out of the way. Once he's certain I'm not hiding any twinges of pain, he brushes a lock of my hair out of my face, his face serious. "Norma, I know we said this before, when you were a little out of it, but I want you to know I mean it with all my heart. I love you, Norma Jean Blackstone."

My breath hitches. I knew I'd said all kinds of weird shit at the hospital, but I remembered telling Zach I love him because it was the truth. The one I'd been too reserved to say. But now, I have no doubts, no worries, which sounds odd, considering my current predicament, but a broken leg doesn't affect my heart in the least. "I love you too, Zachary Thomas Knight."

The moment sparks, and we both smile, the love and light filling us, leaving no room for any shadow of a doubt.

And then Zach bends down and takes my mouth in a kiss and the beautiful light explodes into fiery passion.

Our kiss becomes messy, hungry as we fight for more. "Fuck, Norma," Zach says as he grinds against me, and I moan at the hard ridge of him against my hot pussy. But suddenly, his weight is gone. He stands, ripping his shirt over his head and helping me get my shirt and bra off.

He crouches down, his shoulders between my thighs, one of my knees hooked on the back of the couch and the other bent to let my foot touch the floor. He shoves my skirt up, too inpatient to take it off me since it'd mean rearranging my legs again. Instead, he leaves it puddled around my waist and grips my panties. "You attached to these?"

I shake my head. "Not at all." And with a fierce tug, he rips them from my body, tossing them over his shoulder carelessly because now he has what he really wants. My pussy, spread wide in front of him, juicy with desire for him.

He licks me, devours me, giving no mercy. There's no tease or buildup. It's full-throttle from the first touch, driving me wild. But he holds my hips firmly in place, not letting me move against him. On some level, I know he's doing it so I don't hurt myself, but on the surface, I like him holding me down, making me take his tongue-lashing. "Oh, God, Zach," I cry out, already on the edge in just minutes.

"Come for me, Brat. Come all over my face with your sweet cream so I can get inside you. Fuck, I need inside you." The desperation in his voice commands me to obey, and I fly off into the dark abyss, letting the blackness behind my lids consume me as lightning shoots through my body, making me shake in ecstasy.

Zach stands, and dropping his jeans and boxer briefs at the same time, he kicks his shoes off, nude in an instant. And then he's hovering over me, cock poised at my entrance.

"I love you, Brat."

"I love you too, Zach."

And then he fills me in one stroke, and though my hands aren't tied this time, I have never felt more bound. Connected to this man, to what we have together, silk strands between us and surrounding us, creating something better together than we are alone. Not Norma, not Zach. But *us*.

And as his cock pushes into me, jackhammer hard and fast, he roars as his orgasm rips through him. And the knots in the metaphorical silk binds cinch tighter, just like my pussy as I come again with him.

*T*he Sapphire Bowl isn't the biggest bowl game around, but it is on New Year's Eve, which makes it extra-special. Beyond the obvious football incentives, I've got some bonus motivation sitting at the fifty-yard line. Norma is sitting in her seat, watching my every move, her small body more or less draped in one of my old jerseys. Liam and Arianna sit on her right. My parents sit on her left.

Unsurprisingly, my parents *love* Norma. Norma was nearly gutted when my mom heard us giving each other hell, sure that they'd think we were seriously bickering and an obvious match made in hell. But I knew better, and when my mom had come in the room, she'd addressed Norma first before even giving me a hello kiss, telling her, 'You get him, dear. Keeping a Knight man in line is dang-near a full-time job.' But Norma's been overly sweet ever since, to the point my Dad quietly asked me if the Brat nickname was supposed to be ironic. I assured him that Norma was being extra-sweet because she wanted to make a good impression but was a strong-willed, sassy, prickly brat who kept me on my toes and in my place. And I liked her that way. He'd grinned and told me 'Good job, Son.' I think that was the best compliment he's ever given me, even better than all the football praise he's heaped on my shoulders over the years of playing.

But of course, Norma is sitting instead of standing because of the cast still clunking along on her lower leg. She's almost to Freedom Day, as she calls it, but also known as cast removal day, and she's ready, counting down the days on her calendar. But she's managing pretty well. I, Arianna, and Liam pitch in when she needs something, and her parents helped too until they left a couple of days after Christmas.

I give them all a wave and catch the kiss Norma blows me for luck before turning back to the field. "You feeling it, Zach?" Coach Buckley asks me. "This could be your last game." I can tell he's pumping me for info without asking outright.

I shake my head. "Nope, I haven't told Coach Jefferson yet, but I did a lot of thinking over winter break. I'm coming back next year. I want to be a Raven one more year, finish my degree, and then see about the pros."

Coach Buckley grins. "You haven't told Coach Jefferson yet?"

I chuckle. "Just haven't had a chance with the holidays and practices to be ready for today. Besides, I'm sure you've noticed how nice he's been to me? He thinks I might declare early for the draft and is trying to make me forget about the five AM practices and the two-a-day drills. But I remember, and I'm still staying."

Coach Buckley claps his hands, the sound loud even on the riot of the sideline. "Well, all right, then. Let's play some damn football then!"

To say it's a good game is a ridiculous understatement. We're playing the Jaguars, and while they're a great team, we strike hard and fast. By the end of the first quarter, we've already scored twenty-one points.

"You planning on slowing down?" Coach Buckley asks me as I come off after the third touchdown. "Or are you just trying to shatter the TD record?"

"Not stopping until the game clock hits zero," I reply, grabbing a Gatorade and giving Norma a thumbs-up. She waves a pompom on a stick madly, making me laugh because she's suddenly my favorite fucking groupie ever. Her little cheer gives me new energy, which helps because our defense is struggling and the Jags hit us for two straight long touchdowns.

It becomes a shootout, and as we enter the final two of the fourth quarter, I know the guys are exhausted. Sweat drips off every facemask and every player's chest is heaving. "Okay, let's keep it going. Almost there, guys."

"Zach," one of my linemen says, his white jersey nearly gray with sweat. "There ain't much left in the tank, man."

I want to slap him in the head, tell him to man the fuck up . . . but looking around at the other guys, he's right and just saying what they're all thinking. I'm being fueled by something superhuman, something that they don't have. I have Norma. Chuckling, I nod. "Okay . . . then let's run a Bratty Norma Special."

It's a new play, something we've run once or twice in practice as a 'fuck it, let's have some fun' type shit. The guys grin, and it's my ass if this goes badly.

At the snap, everyone goes directly at and nails the closest Jaguar, looking like something out of a bar fight rather than football. It's chaos, it's anarchy . . . it's just like my girl, fighting on every damn front. And just like in real life, I run through it all, slick and smooth through every obstacle and diversion and battle, like I'm playing Frogger on the Interstate. In seconds, I only have one guy left to beat, Prince Ellsmore, an All-American strong safety who's been gunning for me all game.

"Sorry, Prince, but I'm the fucking King," I growl as I lower my shoulder, hitting him right under the chin. It sends him flying, and I go the rest of the way untouched for a fifty-three-yard touchdown run.

It proves to be the knife in the Jaguars' heart, winning the barn burner with a score of 56-45.

The trophy presentation is a huge event. The Ravens haven't won a bowl game in almost a decade, and Coach Jefferson looks like he's about to cry as he holds it aloft.

"And now the MVP of the Sapphire Bowl," the cable TV host says, bringing out another trophy. "Zach Knight, get up here!"

The crowd's going nuts, but when they stick the mic in

my face, I look down at the trophy, the reality more surreal than every dream I've ever had of this moment.

I try to find my mind, remembering to thank my team and my coaches. I hear the TV host ask about a repeat performance next year, and I smile as I see Norma making her way slowly and carefully through the crowd. The guys notice her too and help her get a front-row seat for my moment because that's what family does, and these guys and Norma are my family, my chosen tribe. "I'd love a repeat of this next year. I'll be here to help make it happen as the starting senior quarterback for the Ravens."

I let my eyes flick to Coach for his reaction, and his jaw is dropped open, and the tears that threatened flow freely now. He closes his mouth and gives me a thumbs-up, a look of pride in his eyes.

And with my interview done, I can finally do what I've been wanting to do since the timer buzzed. I rush to Norma, picking her up and spinning her around in joy. Her tiny hands fist my jersey, and she pulls me into a deep kiss, our lips still smiling even as we try to pucker. The crowd's cheers get even louder.

We part just a bit, and she whisper-yells, "You think you can put up with all this plus me for another year?" A sassy smirk is on her face as she challenges me with those words.

I give her a cocky grin back. "Brat, I'm fucking sure I'm gonna be putting up with you for at least fifty years."

BUCK WILD

THE BENNETT BOYS RANCH

Chapter 1
James

With a squeeze of the snips and a twist of my pliers, I finish one more section of fence. Gazing left, then right, I can see just how much I've done and just how far I have left to go. The answer is the same as the last time I checked. Not enough and too much.

We need this pasture secure before we move the herd over, and that's happening one way or another by the end of the week. Unfortunately, this fence was totally wrecked last winter, and with everything that's happened to the family, it's been put off until the last minute. And it seems that last minute is my new middle name.

I know I need to hurry, but my back needs a break more. This isn't a sprint, the eight seconds of exhilaration and adrenaline that I'm used to. This is still hours of work left, and if I'm not careful, I'll end up useless with miles of fence to go. I stand tall to stretch, raising my arms high above me and lifting my face to the bright sun of the June day.

Taking a deep breath, I can feel the sweat rolling down my face, so I pull my hat off to mop a rag across my brow. It's strange, but in the barely blowing breeze, I can feel my dad's presence, proud that I'm back here, home on the ranch, doing what he always wanted me to do. In the sound of the creek that's just on the other side of this rise I'm working on fencing, it almost sounds like he's chuckling in that way he used to when he knew something would happen even if my brothers and I swore it never would.

His passing is still so new that it sometimes doesn't feel real. Speaking to the refreshing wind at my back, I tuck my rag in my back pocket and adjust my Stetson on my head. "So, you're watching, are you? I know exactly what you're gonna say, Pops. *Fence ain't gonna fix itself, boy. Back to work, only way to get done what needs to be done.* I know, and I'm gonna get it done."

Taking one last deep breath, I let the air current guide me back to the next section, ready to roll for another few hours. It's been hours already, Or maybe minutes. Shit, it's hard to tell when the work is this repetitive. All I know is that I'm in that eternity between my quickly eaten lunch and sunset when I hear hoofbeats coming.

I don't even have to look to know it's my older brother. Especially since both my brothers are older than me and have never let me forget that I'm the baby. But right now, I know it's my oldest brother, coming to check on me like he always does.

Turning to face Mark, I tug the brim of my hat down to shield my eyes from the sun, which is hanging pretty low in the sky. Ah, hours then, not the minutes I'd feared. I've kept up a good pace, the end must be in sight.

"Hey, Mark." I greet with a single lift of my chin.

He reins in his horse Sugarpea, his favorite gelding that he's had since he was a teenager. "Have you been napping out here or something, James? This as far as you've made it? Gonna be some early mornings and late nights to get this pasture prepped in time. Guess it's a good thing you brought the ATV, it'll let you work after dark with those floodlamps."

He makes a *tsking* sound that both irritates me and makes me laugh. I take a closer look around, I've got less than a half mile to go before I reach the corner and today's goal. "Fuck you, man. I'm working my ass off out here while you've been pushing papers around in the barn office. I bet I've earned more sweat in the past half hour than your big ass has sitting in that old swivel chair all day. But don't you worry, I'll be in for dinner."

He smirks at me, leaning onto the horn of his saddle to look down at me with a knowing grin. "Of course you will. I might be a scary fella, but none of us want Mama chasing after us. She's the scariest son of a gun I know."

I twist my face into a fictitious mask of fear, staring behind him with wide eyes. "Oh, you done bought it now!"

Mark spins to look behind him, just as I'd planned, but there's nothing there besides the wide-open acres of golden-green land. "Shit, you had me thinking Mama was right behind me. You been taking acting lessons or something when you're on that rodeo tour?"

I laugh, the gentle shake of my body and lightness in my head feeling good. It's been foreign lately and maybe just what I need. Mark, never being one to laugh, merely smiles, but for him, that's basically the same as laughter, so I'm calling it a win. "You've always been easy to fool. Remember when we were kids and I jumped from the hayloft and faked breaking my leg? You were so scared you damn near pissed your Levis. It don't take being Daniel Day-Lewis to get you."

Mark's mouth thins, but he nods and gives me an evil grin. "Well, I planned to help you with a length of fence, but after that stunt, I'm thinking maybe I'll go on in and have a shower before dinner. Might even prop my feet up and watch some of Mama's shows with her while she gets dinner ready."

My jaw drops; he's so serious that when he plays it straight, it's hard to tell if he's joking or not. "The fuck you will! Get your ass off your high horse and help. Just because the corner's just up ahead don't mean the whole damn fence is done! We've got miles to go and not enough time to do it."

Mark shakes his head, looking a lot older than he really is. Sure, I'm the baby of the group, but Mark isn't that much older. But in the afternoon light, the weight of responsibility hangs on his face so much that he looks like he's pushing forty instead of still two stepping with thirty. "There's never enough time. Hasn't been for a while now."

The silence stretches for a moment, both of us lost in thought of missing Pops. He loved this land, the land he bought on faith, back in the time when everyone was saying old-fashioned family farming and ranching was going the way of bell bottoms and the Marlboro man. He'd been the one who saw what this land could be, a harsh mistress that still loved us back and provided for a man who was willing to use his brains as well as his body and heart to tend it.

He loved us boys, all three of us. He spent every day teaching us how to be men and how to be ranchers. He'd taught me to ride almost as soon as I could walk, to respect the value of a man's hard work, and that sweat was sometimes more valuable than gold. And he taught us to love.

The best example of that was how Pops loved Mama. He would often tell us about how once he saw his Louise, he knew right then and there that he was going to marry that girl. He'd been eighteen at the time.

His passing hit us hard, especially Mark. It was Mark who found Pops, lying just beyond the big elm tree we've got in the front yard, a peaceful look on his face and his hat somehow placed respectfully over his eyes like he was taking a nap.

By everyone's guess, he realized what was coming, the years of hard work and workman's breakfasts catching up to him, and had laid down and sent his horse back to the barn. As soon as Duster nickered at the back door riderless, Mark said he knew something was wrong. It took him awhile to find Pops, but it didn't matter. He could have been faster than the Flash and he would've been too late. When the reaper comes for you, there's never enough time.

Mark found our father lying next to the same tree that he proposed to Mama under thirty-two years ago. We didn't have the years with him we thought we would. I'm back home for now, but only for the long summer. When the fall circuit starts up again, my ass needs to be on the back of a fifteen-hundred-pound pissed-off bull if I want to get my sponsorship checks. I'm not sure how Pops managed to time his unexpected passing with the rodeo schedule he always hated, but since he did, I've got a long stretch of months to stay here, settle in with Mama and my brothers to make the ranch work somehow without Pops' fiercely loving hand guiding us all.

My eyes meet Mark's and he growls, swinging off Sugarpea and tying her off on the back gate of my ATV trailer before bumping my shoulder as he passes by me in a sign of brotherly love that also means "shut the fuck up." Saying nothing, he roots around in the back of the trailer and comes out with another pair of snips. "Okay, James, let's see if we can get all the sections from here to the corner and a few beyond done before dinner. Deal?"

I eye the length of fence, not seeing too much that needs repair. This part of the pasture is in the lee of the rise, and because of that, didn't catch the driving winds that some of the other areas did. "Hell, if it's mostly just inspection, I bet we can do five or six. Let's hit it."

We get to work, side by side, the same way we did for years, words not even needed as we dance around each other, checking each level of wire and all the barbs, careful to scan and fix any weak spots.

We complete our goal, loading up our tools in the back of the ATV just as we hear the ringing of the bell out across the flat land. Mark grins and unties the lead on Sugarpea, swinging up into the saddle easily. "Nice job."

I smile, hopping behind the handlebars of the ATV. "Told you we'd make it. How about I race you to the house. If I win, I get your roll. If you win, you get…"

He interrupts me, already wheeling Sugarpea around. "I get your whole plate."

Before I can even register what he said, he's off and running, Sugarpea tearing up great hunks of turf with every step like Mark's racing him in the Kentucky Derby. I twist the throttle on my ATV, but I'm held back some as I can't just floor it, or else I'd flip the small trailer and send my tools flying everywhere.

Still, it's a race of one horsepower versus twenty-eight, and I'm close on Mark's heels as we get to the barn. He unsaddles and stalls Sugarpea while I unload my tools before we both wash our hands and splash our faces with the cool water from the old-fashioned pump, then go bursting in the back door, still jockeying for position. The race is more about bragging rights than dinner, but make no mistake, Mark will totally take my plate if he wins, and I'll damn sure enjoy that extra roll with lots of moans at how delicious it is to stir the shit if I win.

Our roughhousing catches Mama's attention though, and she turns from the stove, a big wooden spoon in her hand, the same kind that she's threatened to break over my ass if I didn't behave myself. "What the hell are you two doing? Behave yourself in my house, or you'll be eating on the back porch with the dogs. And they don't get dessert."

We sober up, knowing that she's dead serious, but the competitive spirit we've always had doesn't just stop so we discreetly rib each other, daring the other to make a sound and be the loser. Neither of us will ever give in though, and ultimately, we sit at our respective spots at the table. Pops' spot is empty, Mark's is at his left as the eldest son, while Mom will sit at the other end of the table, nearest me. Luke used to sit on Pops' right, but he's adjusted, he'll sit next to Mama.

Mark glances over, removing his hat and hanging it off the back of his chair. "I'm getting your plate tomorrow." He swings two fingers between his eyes and mine, indicating that he's watching me. I grin, and give him the finger. Like hell he will.

Mama turns around in a huff, thankfully slow enough that I can hide my hand. "Mark Thompson Bennett, did you just say you were gonna eat your brother's dinner? You know how hard he works, how hard you all work, and he needs his dinner. You'll do no such thing."

Being the baby in the family is sometimes the most annoying thing in my life, but other times, like this, it's a blessing.

Deciding to needle Mark just a little bit, I rub my stomach, moaning a little. "I'm so fucking hungry. I worked damn hard, I'm almost halfway around the back pasture and didn't have enough lunch because it was too far to come back to the house for a nibble. Is that my favorite pot roast?"

Yeah, I'm laying it on thick, but the hard expression on Mark's face is worth it. He spent most of my life eating the grisly end of pot roasts while I was getting the nice, juicy cuts. No wonder he prefers steak or hamburgers over roast.

Apparently, I overplayed though, as Mama turns around, pointing her spoon at me. "Boy, do I look like a fool? I packed your lunch and you had two big sandwiches in there, so quit needling your brother and just eat. And don't you dare cuss at my dinner table. You might be a grown man, but you're not too big for me to bend you over my knee and remind you of those proper manners I taught you growing up."

Mark smirks at me, the image of our petite mother, who's barely five-foot-two and maybe a buck fifteen soaking wet after Thanksgiving dinner, bending my six-foot-three-inch, two-hundred-pound frame over her knee to deliver a whoopin' quite comical.

I duck my head, putting my hands in my lap. "Sorry ma'am."

Thinking to do what she said and "just eat", I reach for a serving dish of potatoes before feeling eyes on me. Looking up, Mama's eyes are boring into me, and I snatch my hand back so fast my knuckles rap on the edge of the table. "I think those rodeo folks aren't doing you any favors, James. Bunch of wild heathens. You don't start until everyone's at the table."

I sigh, knowing that Mama's right. There are advantages to being a professional rodeo rider, and not waiting on big brothers is one of them. "Where is Luke anyways? He's late."

Mama swats me in the back of the head before I can reach for the potatoes again, clucking her tongue. "He'll be just a minute. He's checking on Briarbelle."

Suitably chastised, I glance up as the backdoor swings open and slams against the frame.

I lean back as Luke, all lanky six-foot-two of him, comes in, his face still streaked with dirt from the barn. "Well, speak of the devil and he shall appear."

He doesn't respond, just turns to the big industrial sink by the back door to wash up, but I see him sneak me a middle finger so I know he heard me. Once he sits, Mama brings the roast over and prays quickly so we can dig in, passing dishes back and forth and filling up our plates.

Dinner is a rowdy affair, full of fast eating, belly pats, and moans of delight when Mama brings out chocolate pudding for dessert. "Now boys, I appreciate all the hard work you're doing... so there's a little bit extra in here tonight for all three of you."

I don't know how she does it, never really thought about it I guess, but she's been feeding the three of us and Pops for decades, every meal delicious and filling and worth all the hard work to earn a place at her table.

It's odd to have the head of the table be empty now, but for the most part, our conversations about the ranch take up enough space to make it feel like Pops is still ghosting about in his vacated chair.

"Make some headway on the fence today, James?" Luke asks.

"If you can imagine it, Mark actually helped a little," I admit. "We got around the far corner and six sections back the other way. It'll be ready."

As we take our empty plates to the sink and rinse them off for the dishwasher just like we were taught, Luke fills us in on Briarbelle, his favorite mare. She's old for a first-time mother, and it's been tough on her.

"Briarbelle is ready to foal, but she's not handling it too well. She's been pacing and sweating all day, and she's already leaking milk. I'll watch her tonight, but I already told Doc to be on alert. He plans to come out bright and early in the morning. I just don't have a good feeling."

Luke is the best of any of us with the horses. There's something about his manner, his mellow presence setting them at ease usually, so him having a bad feeling is tantamount to a prophesy of something being wrong and we know better than to squash it.

Mark dries off his hands, and leans against the big counter in the kitchen, his eyes dark with concern. "Shi… sorry to hear that," he says, still aware of Mama's presence as she scrubs at the roasting pan. Just because dinner is done is no reason to curse in Louise Bennett's kitchen. Clearing his throat, Mark continues. "Need a hand tonight? I can take a shift to watch over her."

Never one to be outshined by my brothers, I speak up. "Me too. Whatever you need."

Luke shakes his head, smiling a little. He's always been the one of us to be sort of solo, not really antisocial but just… private. "Naw, I've got it. She's comfortable with me, and I already got my cot set up so I can rest when I can. But come on out in the morning, nice and easy. Hopefully, we'll have a new foal and both momma and baby will be healthy."

Chapter 2
Sophie

I CAN'T HELP IT, BOUNCING SIDE TO SIDE AS EXCITEMENT courses through my body. It's either bounce or fidget, and I know if I fidget I'm going to end up looking like I need to pee. Actually, I probably look like I need to pee now, but I can't stop.

Who'd have thought a few years ago that a summer internship with a crusty old seen-it-all vet way out in the country would cause this degree of joy in my heart, especially when the sun's not even up yet?

Definitely not me. I'd grown up a city slicker, the sort of girl who was wealthy and never had to worry much because my brother, Jake, always took care of me… and everything. He was a little overbearing at times, but I didn't fault him for it too much.

After all, he didn't ask to be both brother and caretaker. When our parents died and I was barely out of elementary school, he didn't have much choice. But he stepped up and was the best fill-in parent an orphan could have, and I know he worked his ass off to make sure I had a happy life, even when I went through a rough patch in my teen years and gave him more than a fair ration of hell.

But Jake never wavered, never questioned taking me in. It was just the two of us against the world for a lot of years, but he'd met and married the love of his life, Roxy, several years ago and in her, I'd found a friend and sister before going off to college.

My original plan had been to follow Jake's footsteps, attending the same private university he had and getting my business degree before staying on track for my MBA. I figured I could join Jake in business and make oodles of money just like him. And that plan worked through my freshman year, when I took the same old boring English and Math that everyone has to do. But a mess-up in my schedule my sophomore year changed every-thing for me.

I'd filled out my course request for basic biology, an easy A class that would let me check the box before moving on to my business courses. But one typo in the computer, and I found myself in Animal Studies, and no matter what I tried with the counselor, it was just too late to switch.

So, I resigned myself to studying dogs and cats and rabbits for a semester. Considering I'd never even had a pet, the experience was eye-opening and... amazing. Somehow, in the sixteen weeks of that intro class, my whole life changed. Getting to see the wonderful tapestry that is life on this planet up close, it touched me in a way that all of the money Jake had in the bank just... didn't.

I changed my major from business to pre-veterinary studies and never looked back, spending the next three years learning all about animals, big and small. My semester with large farm animals was my absolute favorite, following our John Wayne-esque mentor around on his ranch, checking on his cattle, administering vaccines, and doing wellness checks before they went to market.

I did a summer internship with him to prolong my learning, and that's when he taught me to ride horses. I loved the freedom of riding, feeling the wind in my face and a powerful beast beneath me, willing to cede control and go where I led.

It was exhilarating and I felt honored to experience it. It was then that I knew my specialty as a vet would be large ranch animals. The more time I can spend on wide-open land, keeping the herds and horses healthy, the happier I'll be. Not that I don't mind deworming a dog or spaying a cat, but there's something about the large animals that call to me.

Jake and Roxy have been supportive, if a little confused by the drastic change I've gone through in the last few years. I think Jake is wondering if I've had a brain transplant. For the most part, they're still living a jetsetter, urban trend-setter life and as happy as I am for them, I want something different.

Which is why I'm bouncing around on my toes now,

looking more like I'm getting ready to fight Ronda Rousey than go to work. I officially graduated two weeks ago, my bachelor's degree in hand and my invitation to vet school is pinned to the refrigerator in the small house I rented for the summer.

Sure, I could sit on my ass and take a couple of breather months before jumping into my vet courses, but I'm too much like Jake. I want to *do*. So I found a summer job in an area where I can be close-ish to my support people, but far enough away that I can stand on my own two feet.

I was lucky enough, and damn well qualified, to snag a summer internship working with a local vet named Doc Jones. It's a perfect fit, really. He's well-versed in every-thing animal related, having likely seen it all and done it all at least once, while I bring what he calls "fresh air" to the office. Better than that, he's actually a really great teacher, willing to share his knowledge and help me be ready for a career with big animals.

Like today, the reason I'm bouncing. Doc got a call last night, and this morning we're doing a wellness check on a foaling horse at a ranch way outside of town. A lot better than what I'd expected, which was preparing two thousand doses of vaccine for a local sheep rancher. I'm sure I'll be sticking sheep in the ass at some point this week, but seeing a live birth? That'll get me standing here on the curb outside my tiny house in town, two insulated cups of coffee in hand and a thermos of caffeine nectar in my bag at my feet.

It's nice and crisp right now, but it's supposed to be hot as balls today. Even so, I need my morning coffee fix, and Doc Jones *definitely* does. I hear him coming long before I actually see him, his old as hell GMC pickup squealing to a stop in front of me. He looks like he always does, sort of a cross between Sam Elliot and DeForest Kelley, which I guess is appropriate. "Hop in," he says, reaching over and pulling up the old-fashioned lock on his passenger door. "I just talked to the boy at the ranch and Briarbelle's foal still isn't here. If we hustle, we'll get to see her deliver. You seen that yet?"

I nod, sliding in and handing Doc his coffee. "Oh yeah. Actually, I've seen four deliveries. But they were pretty by the book, only one needed a minor assist."

"Well, I'm thinking this might not be as textbook. Hope you don't mind some funk.

I shake my head, sipping at my coffee. "I don't mind. It's always amazing to see, it's such a miracle every time."

I know my eyes are sparkling with anticipation because I'm not just blowing smoke, I really do love to see the miracle and make sure mom and baby are okay.

Doc looks over at me, studying me. "Eager, aren't ya?"

"Come on Doc," I complain a little. "Aren't you just as excited?"

He laughs and pushes the gas on his old truck a little harder. He could afford a new one, but I think he's determined to run this thing to the half million mile mark before he'll feel like he's gotten his money's worth. "Well, I've done this a few more than four times, but I reckon it's always a sight to see."

As we drive out, Doc quizzes me on what I'm likely to

see, what I need to be concerned about, procedures if this happens, what about if that happens, and more. I nail every single one of them, and as he turns down the last road, he gives me a satisfied grunt. "That'll do, Miss Sophie. That'll do just fine."

I can feel the blush on my cheeks at his praise, pleased to have answered his questions correctly. This might be just a summer job, but I want to be the best at it.

Doc gives me a half smile and makes another little grunt, patting the dashboard.

Get the Full Book HERE!

ABOUT THE AUTHOR

Join my mailing list and receive 2 FREE ebooks!

Other Books By Lauren

The Virgin Diaries:
Satin and Pearls || Leather and Lace || Silk and Shadows

Irresistible Bachelors **(Interconnecting standalones):**
Anaconda || Mr. Fiance || Heartstopper
Stud Muffin || Mr. Fixit || Matchmaker
Motorhead || Baby Daddy || Untamed

Get Dirty **(Interconnecting standalones):**
Dirty Talk || Dirty Laundry || Dirty Deeds

Bennett Boys Ranch:
Buck Wild

Connect with Lauren Landish.
www.laurenlandish.com
admin@laurenlandish.com

facebook.com/lauren.landish

twitter.com/laurenlandish

instagram.com/lauren_landish

19472753R00124

Printed in Great Britain
by Amazon